"I Won't Let You Use Me, Matt!

You know there is absolutely nothing between us."

"I know no such thing. I remember that kiss behind the palms in the moonlight. No woman kisses a man like that unless she has a deep feeling for the man she is kissing."

"Perhaps it was just the mood of the evening." Cara tried to ignore the tingle in the hollow of her back. "Anyone can grow romantic when there is moonlight and wine and the scent of roses all around—"

ELLEN GOFORTH,
a woman of many talents, combines music, teaching and professional writing. She plays piano and trumpet and has published extensively for adults and children. The lush and exotic settings in her delightful novels are drawn from personal experience.

Dear Reader:

During the last year, many of you have written to Silhouette telling us what you like best about Silhouette Romances and, more recently, about Silhouette Special Editions. You've also told us what else you'd like to read from Silhouette. With your comments and suggestions in mind, we've developed SILHOUETTE DESIRE.

SILHOUETTE DESIREs will be on sale this June, and each month we'll bring you four new DESIREs written by some of your favorite authors—Stephanie James, Diana Palmer, Rita Clay, Suzanne Stevens and many more.

SILHOUETTE DESIREs may not be for everyone, but they are for those readers who want a more sensual, provocative romance. The heroines are slightly older—women who are actively invloved in their careers and the world around them. If you want to experience all the excitement, passion and joy of falling in love, then SILHOUETTE DESIRE is for you.

I'd appreciate any thoughts you'd like to share with us on new SILHOUETTE DESIRE, and I invite you to write to us at the address below:

Karen Solem
Editor-in-Chief
Silhouette Books
P.O. Box 769
New York, N.Y. 10019

ELLEN GOFORTH
A New Dawn

Silhouette Romance

Published by Silhouette Books New York

America's Publisher of Contemporary Romance

Other Silhouette Books by Ellen Goforth

Path of Desire

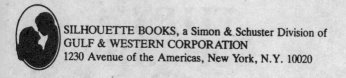

SILHOUETTE BOOKS, a Simon & Schuster Division of
GULF & WESTERN CORPORATION
1230 Avenue of the Americas, New York, N.Y. 10020

Chapter One

Cara Logan smoothed her pencil-slim skirt over one knee and tasted the tart sweetness of the last sip of sherry in her crystal goblet as she waited for her aunt to join her for lunch. Although she had freshened up in the ladies' room, she still felt tired and rumpled from her long plane flight from Chicago and from the limo ride from Houston. July. It sapped one's vitality.

"Another drink, Miss Logan?" A waitress wearing a sea-blue sheath that matched the decor of the dining room stood at her elbow.

Cara peered at her glass, surprised that it was empty. "Yes, please. Another sherry."

How she hated waiting here alone. She shuffled her feet, feeling her heels sink into the plush carpet. People would think she didn't have a friend to lunch with. Cara scowled at that thought, remembering

the times back in high school when sometimes she
hadn't had a friend to lunch with. She had been new
in Galveston. And she had been so shaken by her
parents' divorce that she had found it hard to make
friends. How much she owed to Aunt Estelle for
taking her in that year!

In moments the waitress set the sparkling sherry
in front of her on the pale blue cloth. "You're Estelle
LaDeaux's niece, right?"

"Yes." Cara inhaled a mouth-watering aroma of
seafood which escaped from the kitchen.

"Your aunt just telephoned, Miss Logan. She'll be
here shortly. She was delayed on business."

"Thank you," Cara said.

"Think you'll like Galveston?" the waitress asked.
"Estelle told me you're from Chicago."

"Yes, I'm sure I'll like Galveston." Cara smiled at
the waitress. "It isn't as if I'm seeing the island for
the first time, though. I grew up in Chicago, but I
spent my senior year of high school here with Aunt
Estelle."

"Your aunt decorated this place," the waitress
said. "That's when she and I first met. She's quite a
gal."

Cara hid a smile, thinking how few people would
dare call *the* Estelle LaDeaux a gal.

"The Blue Lagoon." Cara studied the posh,
dimly-lighted restaurant Aunt Estelle had chosen for
their welcome-home meeting. Shadowed mirrors
like rectangles of satin smoke reflected the glow of
the candles set in hurricane globes. Subtly sculp-
tured carpeting covered the floor and a textured
paper covered the walls, the monochromatic blues
making a perfect foil for the oyster-colored rattan

furniture. The restaurant was like her aunt, sophisticated, highly polished and flawless in appearance.

"Interiors planned by the House of LaDeaux always possess an unmistakable charm, don't they?" Cara asked, since the waitress was still lingering. "I love all these shades of blue. The cobalt floor covering reminds me of the deep-sea blues off the coast, and the aquamarine walls catch the color of the shallow waters near the shoreline."

The waitress looked up at the ceiling. "And talk about sky blue. You got it up there. It's almost like being outdoors. And do you know, Estelle wouldn't let us drape shrimp nets and conch shells on the walls. Even though this is a seafood house, Estelle said the nets and shells were a cliché. Don't know exactly what she meant, but I like the walls hung with seascapes. My own nephew painted one of them. Estelle believes in giving young artists a chance."

Now the waitress smiled and hurried off to serve two women whom the hostess had seated nearby. Cara glanced at her watch, then held it to her ear. Yes, it was running. Aunt Estelle was already twenty minutes late. Cara pulled a slim volume from her bulging shoulder purse. *The Gay Nineties*. Aunt Estelle had sent it to her last week for her twenty-third birthday. A strange gift, yet maybe not so strange. Since Aunt Estelle usually had good reasons for everything she did, there must be a reason for the book. Cara could only wonder what it might be.

She began to read, unmindful of the chatter of the two women at the next table until one of them lowered her voice to a stage whisper that carried more clearly than her normal tone.

"Just look who's coming in, Bertie. I've heard she *always* dresses that way."

Cara exercised great willpower to keep from turning to ogle the new arrival.

"If I were as rich as a bank, I'd have me a car to match every dress I owned," the other woman said. "All that scarlet is a bit much, don't you think? Why, she's sixty if she's a day."

"On her scarlet is perfect. Sets off that platinum hair, that svelte figure."

Cara felt herself blushing as she realized the women were talking about Aunt Estelle. A moment later she noted the chagrined expressions on their faces as Estelle LaDeaux bore directly toward them, then eased past them to give Cara a hug and a kiss. The scent of her musky perfume permeated the air.

"Let me look you over," Aunt Estelle said, slipping gracefully into the chair across the table from Cara. "You've changed in five years, my dear. For the better, I might add. I knew you'd learn to let that black hair of yours hang to your shoulder in a straight fall. And those bangs set off your dark eyes to full advantage. Obsidian. Your eyes always have reminded me of polished obsidian." Aunt Estelle cocked her head like a listening gull and studied Cara a moment longer. "And I'd say you've added a few pounds in all the right places too."

Cara squirmed, embarrassed at all the attention. "*You're* looking well too, Aunt Estelle." Cara glanced at her aunt's scarlet ankle-length sheath which was her trademark. "You haven't changed a bit."

"At least not on the outside," Aunt Estelle said. "However, the doc says there are some changes on the inside. That's why I'm so pleased that you decided to return to Galveston. I need you, Cara. And I hope we need each other."

Cara leaned forward, frowning slightly in concern. It was hard to imagine her hard-driving aunt not at the peak of physical condition. "Is it quite serious? Your illness, I mean."

"A little heart murmur now and then. A little high blood pressure." Estelle shrugged. "Doc says I should slow down."

"Then you must do as he says."

"It's been hard to slow down with so much work to be done, but now that you're here to help out I know I'll be able to relax a bit. I'm counting on you, Cara. House of LaDeaux is counting on you."

"Are you ladies ready to order?" the waitress asked, poising her pencil above her order pad.

"We'll have the usual, Annabell," Estelle said. "Lobster salad supreme, minted tea and your special buttered hot rolls."

Cara sighed, remembering Aunt Estelle's authoritative ways, but today she didn't object. She was tired from summer school finals, tired from her trip, ready to let someone else make decisions for her. And besides, she loved lobster supreme and hot rolls.

"Did someone die?" Aunt Estelle asked suddenly.

"What do you mean?"

"I'm referring to your somber black suit." Estelle blinked, trying to hide the twinkle in her eyes. "Looks like you're headed for a funeral instead of for the start of a grand new career."

"Black is considered quite chic in the city." Cara masked her inner qualms with a firm voice. She had learned she could hide a lot of insecurity behind a well-tailored suit.

"We'll find something more suitable for you to wear here," Estelle said. "You'll want to establish a personal trademark just as I have done with my scarlet sheaths. Clothes are the first thing one person notices about another, so I think that's a good starting place. What about a jumpsuit? Maybe in a leopard-print satin. That would be eye-catching, something everyone would remember."

"Aunt Estelle, don't you ever get tired of wearing the same thing every day?"

"Of course not. I have a dozen scarlet sheaths. The fabrics are different. Silk. Chiffon. Satin."

"But they all look about the same."

"That's the idea. A trademark is something the public remembers. I like wearing the same style dress. It eliminates the everyday decision about what to wear. It leaves my mind free to think about more important things like House of LaDeaux."

Cara had a butterfly-in-the-stomach feeling. Why was she always so unsure of herself? Oh, to have some of Aunt Estelle's dash and self-confidence! If Aunt Estelle ever had butterflies in her stomach, she would have them flying in formation in no time at all. Cara knew she had to develop self-confidence to present a strong exterior to the world.

"Cara?" Estelle looked at Cara, her head again tilted to one side. "Are you absolutely sure you want to come back to Galveston? For two years, I mean?"

"But of course I do. I've been dreaming of this job ever since I received your invitation. I've been looking forward to being here, anticipating the challenge of working for you, planning a career for myself."

"Two years can be a long time. I hope you don't

think I'm being unfair in requiring you to sign a two-year contract with me."

Cara sipped her tea, enjoying the minty fragrance and taste, then she smiled. "Of course you're not unfair, Aunt Estelle. You can't afford to train me and then have me leave you in a few months. I signed the contract quite willingly."

"Then I know you won't regret signing, Cara. But there's method in my demands. I could have helped you through school, but I didn't. Did you ever wonder why?"

Cara laid her fork down and looked directly at her aunt. "The thought never crossed my mind. It gave me a sense of accomplishment to work my way through the interior decorating course. I knew Hank could never afford to sent me to school with his on-again-off-again actor's salary. And it's all Mom can do to support herself now that she and Hank have divorced. I expected to work my way through school."

"And that's one of the reasons I've asked you to join House of LaDeaux. You've shown a determination to succeed. Now I'll help all I can. We'll help each other. I need you as badly as you need me."

"I'm determined to succeed and to build a career for myself and never to get trapped in domesticity as Mom was."

"You're young to be mapping out your whole life, Cara."

"Well, that's how it's going to be. No men for Cara. I try not to be bitter about Hank leaving us, but it still hurts." Cara started to say more, but the waitress approached again.

"Do you care for dessert?"

Cara watched the way her aunt straightened in her chair, sucked in her stomach, and studied the ceiling for a moment. Then she looked at the waitress. "We'll have banana splits, Annabell. Whipped cream shot with chocolate and two cherries, okay?"

Annabell raised an eyebrow as she smiled. "Yes, ma'am."

After Annabell left Cara laughed. "How did you know I hadn't outgrown my liking for banana splits?"

"Some things one never outgrows. I still love them too." Then Estelle grew serious. "Cara, I'm planning a party for you. A bash to introduce you to all the right people in the Galveston-Houston area."

"The right people?" Cara raised an eyebrow.

"Don't get me wrong. It's not totally a society snob affair. It'll just be a party where you'll meet other decorators, buyers and suppliers. I want people to know that House of LaDeaux has a new associate, so of course, there'll be some society people present."

"When will the party be?" Cara asked, not sure she was going to enjoy being on exhibition.

"I was considering two weeks from today. That would give us time to get you some proper clothes fitted and made. We'll have to call on a designer soon."

"That'll cost a mint. I mean, I'm not—"

"The cost will be to House of LaDeaux. The big problem right now is to find the right place to hold the party. We have to decide that before the invitations can go out."

"The party sounds exciting, Aunt Estelle, but when will I begin work? I'm eager to get started on a real project, not on some beginner's busy work."

"And a real project is exactly what I have planned for you."

"Oh, Aunt Estelle! What is it?" Cara leaned forward, almost upsetting her tea glass.

"For starters, stop calling me Aunt. Okay? It will sound more professional if you just call me Estelle."

"I'll try to remember Au—Estelle."

"That's better."

The banana splits arrived and Estelle ate both cherries and a spoonful of whipped cream before she continued. "Cara, I'm placing you in charge of redecorating Oleander House. I know you can handle it. I'll be available for consultation whenever you feel the need, but you'll be in charge of the project."

Cara laid her spoon down, giving Estelle her full attention. "But what is Oleander House? A flower shop?"

"Oleander House is an old Victorian mansion on Sealy Street." Estelle reached over and tapped the cover of the book Cara had laid beside her plate. "Have you read this?"

"Not yet. I mean I've had exams and all and—"

"You needn't explain. Just read it soon. It will give you background details on the Victorian period. Oleander House was built in 1890. The construction is sound. Your job will be to redecorate the mansion, to bring it back to its turn-of-the-century elegance. Think you can handle that?"

Cara hesitated only a moment, quashing the inner qualms that were making her hands tremble. "Of course I can handle it. I'll read. I'll study. And I know I'll love working with the richly textured fabrics of that period. Who is your client?"

"Mr. Mathewson Daniels."

Cara racked her brain trying to place the name.

"Mathewson Daniels—that sounds vaguely familiar, Estelle, but—"

"It should sound familiar. Daniels is a well-established name in Texas. Mathewson's father founded the Daniels Building Supply enterprise years ago. Mathewson still manufactures and sells building materials. A few years ago he developed a special line of hurricane shutters that have been highly successful."

"Is Mr. Daniels in residence at Oleander House?" Cara asked.

"In a way." Estelle chuckled. "He really didn't plan to be."

"Just how could a millionaire businessman be in residence in a Victorian mansion without planning to be?"

The waitress brought their check on a silver tray. Estelle laid a twenty-dollar bill on the tray and nodded. "Keep the change, Annabell." Then she turned her attention back to Cara.

"Mr. Daniels' regular business office is on The Strand, but many businessmen there are renovating their buildings. The area has become a tourist attraction. A century ago The Strand was called the Wall Street of the Southwest and some of the buildings date back to the mid 1800s."

Cara nodded. "I know the street. But so many of those buildings have been damaged by fire and flood and hurricane. I can't imagine . . ."

"You'll be surprised at the changes that have taken place. A major effort is under way to recycle the old buildings, adapt them to current needs. Mathewson Daniels is doing his bit. While his building is under repair he's had to move his office, just the paperwork part of the business."

"That must have been a lot of bother."

"It was. And it was hard to find temporary quarters. Mr. Daniels surprised everyone when he bought Oleander House and set his temporary office in the third floor ballroom. By using dividing screens he has made the area suit his needs."

"I'll be working on the redecorating while Mr. Daniels' business office is still on the third floor?"

Estelle shoved her chair back and stood, preparing to leave. "Yes. But you'll start your work on the ground floor and progress upward. By the time you're ready to do the ballroom, Mr. Daniels should be relocated on The Strand. Shall we go? I have an appointment in just a few minutes."

Cara pictured Mathewson Daniels. Sixtyish. Balding. Paunchy. A self-satisfied millionaire enjoying his inherited fortune.

"Mr. Daniels plans to move into Oleander House when the renovation is finished?" Cara asked.

"No. Mr. Daniels wants everything finished for his mother's birthday in January—in six months. The house is to be her birthday gift. At least that's what he tells me. I've heard rumors that he's fixing the place up for a lady friend, but I'm reluctant to listen to that kind of gossip."

"Some people are like fountains, Estelle. They keep recirculating rumors as long as they make a pleasing splash."

Estelle laughed. "Mathewson told me his mother grew up in such a house here in Galveston and that she admires the architecture of that period. She lives in New York with her daughter's family, and Mathewson is using the house to entice her back home."

As Cara followed Estelle to the foyer of the

restaurant where they picked up her bag from the coat-check room, she revised her mental picture of Mathewson Daniels. Perhaps he was only in his fifties if his mother was still living and active—or even if he was planning to use Oleander House as a love nest.

Outside the Blue Lagoon the air felt like a damp blanket against Cara's face. She squinted, then slipped on dark glasses. Estelle led the way across a small parking lot to the scarlet Mercedes parked in the fringy shade of a palm tree. Inhaling the salt-scented air, Cara eased her suitcase onto the back seat then slid onto the leather cushion up front beside her aunt. She could sense passersby watching them, or rather watching Estelle in her dress that matched her car. House of LaDeaux. Estelle was a flamboyant advertisement for her business.

"What sort of a man is Mathewson Daniels?" Cara asked. "Will he be easy to work for?"

Estelle hesitated a moment before answering, swung the Mercedes into the fast flow of traffic crossing the causeway onto Galveston Island, then drove at minimum speed as they gazed across the bottle-green waters of the bay.

"I've known Mr. Daniels a long time, Cara. He can be a bit testy at times, but he respects competence. I think the two of you will get along with no problems."

Estelle drove along Broadway toward the beach in the far distance and Cara sat silently drinking in the scene. Pink-blooming oleanders grew in the median, and on either side of the street oak-shaded mansions reminded her of old men at rest, watching the ongoing scene. After they passed the Texas Heroes

Monument and turned onto Sheridan Avenue, Cara spoke up.

"Where are we going? You haven't moved, have you?"

Estelle looked at Cara with a sidelong glance. "I'm taking you straight to Oleander House. You'll be living there."

Cara tried to hide her surprise. "But I thought. I mean—"

"I had planned for you to live with me until you found an apartment of your own," Estelle said. "Then I approached Mathewson Daniels with this grand idea of your living right at Oleander House. There's plenty of room. You can stand a few rent-free months, can't you?"

"I'll be there all alone?"

"Don't worry. A bedside telephone's in and hooked up. I'll be just a ring away. Living in the mansion will help you develop a feeling for the place, and this will help you with the decisions you'll be making about the decor."

Now they had turned onto Sealy Street and Estelle inched the Mercedes along so Cara could study the houses in the neighborhood. Stone. Brick. Frame. The homes had one thing in common. They were holdovers from another era.

Estelle stopped at a white frame mansion set behind black iron fencing which had been cast in a fleur-de-lis design. Oleander House reigned on a corner lot and it was further set apart from its neighbors by a corner entrance rather than an entrance that paralleled the street. With its blue slate roof and its sturdy foundation stones it was like a blue-haired dowager in arch-preserver shoes waiting for the cotillion to begin. Lacy lattice work decorated the wraparound veranda, and each window frame curved in a gothic arch. Cara counted seven gables, one with a stained-glass window.

Estelle parked the Mercedes, and as Cara pulled her suitcase from the back seat, the front door of Oleander House opened. A rangy man with sun-bronzed skin that matched the tan of his Calvin Klein shirt and slacks stepped onto the veranda and hurried down the sandstone steps to greet them. Cara guessed him to be in his early thirties. She was immediately fascinated by his lion's mane of tawny-colored hair that grew back from his forehead, its sun-bleached highlights matching the gold frames of his sunglasses. How like her own father he looked!

"Matt!" Estelle exclaimed, getting from the car to greet him. "How nice that you're here. You're just in time to meet my niece and new associate, Cara Logan. Cara this is the Mathewson Daniels I've been telling you about."

Cara's heart thudded as Mathewson Daniels scrutinized her from head to toe, then scowled, his gaze returning to Estelle. Cara felt herself blushing. She could sense hostility in this man and yet Estelle was calling him Matt. Why had her aunt led her to believe Mathewson Daniels was elderly? Or had she just assumed he was elderly? She couldn't remember.

"Matt, I'm late for an appointment. Do be a dear and carry Cara's bag to her room. And I'd appreciate it if you'd show her through the house."

"Of course, Estelle. But, I must admit, you have caught me by surprise. I had quite naturally assumed that a woman with your business acumen had chosen a more mature woman as your associate."

If Estelle heard this comment, she decided to

ignore it. Glancing at her watch, she inquired quickly, "Her room is ready, isn't it?" and slipped back into the car.

"Naturally, the room is ready. I had Jass see to that."

"Then run along with Matt, Cara. I'll call you later." Estelle waved blithely and drove off before Cara could protest.

Jass! As if by reflex Cara's hand clenched into a fist. He had to mean Jass Whitney. There couldn't be two people with a name like that. Cara tried not to think of her high school rival. So Mathewson Daniels was married. But what difference could that make to her? She was here to help Aunt Estelle and if her job required her to deal with this surly man, she would carry it off with style.

"Come, Miss Logan. I'll show you inside." Then, as if remembering Estelle's request, Matt took Cara's bag from her. As she felt his warm fingers graze hers she drew her hand away so quickly he almost dropped the bag. She felt blood rush to her face and realized he knew that she was shying away from his touch.

Cara watched the way Matt Daniels' muscles rippled under his sport shirt as he carried her heavy bag. Inside the house she breathed deeply, inhaling the musty, closed-for-a-long-time smell. Now she was so close to Matt Daniels she could notice a leathery scent about his person. He led them up a wide stairway, stopping at the first door to the left of the central hallway.

"This will be your suite, Miss Logan."

She stared at the doorway, questions flooding through her mind. Testy? That was the word Estelle had used, wasn't it? Why didn't she level with me

about Mr. Daniels? And just how did she describe
me to him? He almost went into shock when we
were introduced.

Mr. Daniels walked through an office-sitting room
and into a bedroom where he thumped Cara's
suitcase onto the floor. "Take a good look around
before I leave, Miss Logan. If there's anything else
you'll be needing, I'll see that you have it right
away."

Cara forced thoughts of Estelle and of Jass Whitney to the back of her mind and assessed her new
living quarters. The wide pine boards on the bedroom floor were painted a tobacco-spit brown, but
an Oriental carpet covered most of the area. The
faded blue walls melted into the background as Cara
admired the white froth of Priscilla curtains cascad-
ing from gracefully curved rods. A breeze rustled
the leaves of a linden outside the window and a wren
perched on one branch as if posing for a still life.

Bringing her attention back inside the room, she
noted the dresser, chest and bed of polished mahogany. The Tiffany shade on the bedside lamp matched
the shade on the overhead light, and Cara saw a
similar shade on the light in a combination closet-
dressing room.

"I'm sure you'll enjoy this." Matt Daniels opened
another door to reveal a bathroom where a fluffy
throw rug the color of smoked almonds covered
most of the amber and white tile floor. A sunken tub
with golden faucets shaped like mermaids dominated
one side of the room and a fresh scent of honeysuck-
le hung near an oval-shaped bar of soap in the
golden soap dish.

"Mr. Daniels!" Cara stared. "This is Victorian?"

"The original builder had grandiose ideas," Matt

said. "I think he copied this bath from something French—a bath Napoleon had built for Josephine, perhaps."

Reluctant to spend more time in the boudoir with Matt Daniels, Cara stepped into the outer room they had first entered.

"Where did all this furniture come from, Mr. Daniels? I notice that most of the rooms are empty."

"These pieces are demonstrators from Estelle's shop. She's tried to decorate your bedroom in keeping with the period to help you develop a feeling for the project."

Now Cara studied the combination office-sitting room outfitted in very modern decor. A slight odor of lemon-scented furniture polish hinted that someone recently had been at work. Jass? She had a hard time imagining Jass with rag and polish. Jass probably hired someone to take care of menial chores.

A black sectional couch dominated one wall, and two amber-colored easy chairs sat at either end of a Plexiglas coffee table. On the other side of the room a polished walnut desk and a steel file cabinet gave the room a crisp businesslike atmosphere.

"This will be your temporary office, Miss Logan. I've ordered some portable shelves to be installed tomorrow. Estelle says you'll need them for storage space when fabric swatches, floor samples and wallpaper books begin to come in."

"Estelle has thought of everything. I can hardly wait to begin work."

Mr. Daniels gave Cara two heavy iron keys on a leather thong. "This roundheaded key will fit all the doors in this suite. The square-headed key opens the front door downstairs."

Cara took the keys, feeling their cool weight in her hand.

He glanced at his watch. "I'll be leaving now, Miss Logan. I'll keep in touch."

Cara listened to Matt's step on the stairs then she watched from the window until his Porsche disappeared around the corner. Slipping out of her black suit and undergarments she stretched out across the bed and closed her eyes as she thought of the many questions she had for Estelle. A gentle breeze blowing through the window cooled her as it carried the scent of salt and sea and oleander. Yet her eyelids felt warm, and on the back side of them she could see an after-image of Matt Daniels.

She listened to slivers of wrensong from the linden as she drowsed for a few moments, then she rose and hoisted her suitcase onto the bed. Better unpack. Let the wrinkles hang out. No telling what plans Estelle had made for the weekend.

Cara opened her bag and shook out a white jersey robe that would set off the tan she hoped to get now that she was near the beach. She eased into the robe, pulling the sash into a loose knot at her waist, feeling the silky fabric like a cool caress on her skin.

Unpacking didn't take long. She had planned for the black suit to be the mainstay of her work wardrobe. She hung three mix-and-match blouses beside it then unfolded the saffron-colored shirtwaist that seemed right for business occasions. She would add to her wardrobe, following Estelle's suggestions.

Cara jumped as a demanding knock sounded on the door of her suite. Was Estelle here? Flinging open the door, she looked up and up into Matt Daniels' ice blue eyes.

"Is there something I can help you with, sir?"

Suddenly Cara was conscious of her filmy robe with
nothing underneath and her bare-foot sandals.
Clearly she had to keep up a more professional
appearance if she hoped to earn Mr. Daniels' respect. But, after all, she wasn't on duty yet. Cara
smiled, hoping Matt Daniels would look at nothing
but her face.

"I find I have time to show you the rest of the
house now, Miss Logan. Since you've had time to
settle in—"

Cara glanced at her watch. "I've been inside
Oleander House all of fifty-five minutes, Mr. Daniels. I hardly consider that ample time to settle in,
but if there's something special—"

"There is. I've decided that I'd better be with you
when you take your first look at this mansion. I want
you to know what I see and feel so you can adjust
your thinking to mine."

Cara squelched a quick retort. This was her boss.
Her future depended on him. She forced a smile.
"Please have a seat while I change into something
more appropriate for a house tour."

To her surprise Matt Daniels locked his thumb and
forefinger around her wrist. She felt gooseflesh rise
on her upper arm.

"I'm not interested in your personal apparel, Miss
Logan." His gaze traveling boldly over her figure
belied his words. "Do come along without delaying.
I want to guide your thinking about Oleander House
right from the start."

Chapter Two

Arrogant. Cara forced another smile and pulled the sash at her waist a bit tighter. As she held herself very straight so the robe wouldn't gap at the neckline she felt the sleek jersey cling to her breasts and her hips. The clerk had said the robe was elegant enough to double as a hostess gown, but Cara had trouble imagining herself playing hostess for Matt Daniels.

"We'll start our tour downstairs," Matt said. "Come along."

Cara walked abreast of Matt to the stairway, conscious of the catlike grace of his movements. Then he stood aside and let her go first although the stairs were wide enough to accommodate them both. All the way down the steps Cara felt Matt's eyes scrutinizing her every movement. By the time they reached the first floor central hallway her palms were damp and she felt warmer than the day warranted.

"You'll notice that the general floor plan of the mansion centers on this wide hallway both upstairs and down," Matt said. "On the left of the hallway we have this large, formal parlor." Now Matt cupped his hand around Cara's elbow, guiding her. Cara felt the warmth of his touch flow through her whole arm and again she was conscious of the leather scent that traveled with Matt. The room smelled of crumbling plaster and decay. Cara made no comment, but she dropped her arm to her side, leaving no elbow to be cradled. She felt a coolness where his hand had been.

"To the right of the central hallway we have a smaller parlor, the formal dining room and the kitchen." Matt led the way through the rooms. Their footsteps echoed hollowly against the bare floors and Cara tasted a grittiness that rose from the dusty boards.

"It will be your job to determine the various kinds of wood underneath all this paint," Matt said. "In some cases more paint may be in order, but in other cases, the paint hides oak, walnut or mahogany and should be stripped down to its original elegance."

"Perhaps you know more about wood than I do," Cara said.

"Right, but I'm not hunting for a do-it-yourself project. The interior woods and their finishes are your problem. I'm merely stating what I want you to do about them."

"Yes sir." Cara hadn't meant to sound curt, but Matt Daniels' next words warned her that she had.

"Miss Logan, would it be possible for us to be a little less formal? You may call me Matt if I may call you Cara."

"Perhaps that would be best," Cara agreed. She

heard her words come out like the clinking of ice cubes, but she needed that cold aloofness to protect herself. Why did she feel so vulnerable? Cara. Matt Daniels made the name sound very special. Did he know that a direct translation of the word meant dear one? Surely nobody but her mother was aware of that. Anyway, he probably preferred a name with a little more zing—Jass, for instance.

"All right, Cara. Now let's go back upstairs and analyze the personalities of the boudoir suites. But before we go, note this fantastic stairway." Matt paused at the bottom of the stairs, gazing upward. "What does it remind you of?"

"A wedding." Cara blurted the first words that flashed into her mind as if Matt were a psychologist giving her a test that would probe her innermost feelings. Perhaps she had seen too many movies, but whenever she saw a broad stairway in an elegant old home, she pictured a wedding scene with the bride descending the steps in on off-white gown with a satin train flowing behind her like cream against the dark wood.

Matt snorted. "You women all have weddings on the brain!"

"And what does the stairway remind you of?" Cara asked, sorry to have revealed private thoughts to this impossible man.

"I'm redecorating this house for my mother, Cara. I picture her walking down the stairs in a flowing hostess gown, smiling and greeting her distinguished guests."

"Of course," Cara murmured. "I'm sure your mother will be fascinated by the stairway."

"You needn't be sarcastic. Once this staircase is

refinished it will be a showpiece not only in this house but in all of Galveston."

"I wasn't being sarcastic."

"Your voice sounded sarcastic."

"I think you hardly know me well enough to judge that."

Matt looked at her like a lion who had just overpowered its prey then decided it wasn't hungry. "I knew it."

"You knew what?"

"I knew that some little sassbox just out of college would not be a suitable person to take charge of redecorating an elegant mansion."

Cara stood speechless. Nobody had ever called her sassy before. Sassbox. She liked the idea. It was a whole lot better than being called shy. She had heard that word so often it was permanently etched in her brain. But sassbox!

"I'm sorry," Matt said. "I've offended you. I'm sorry."

Cara almost did a double take. "You're forgiven, Mr. Daniels." Again her voice sounded stiff, like that of a college senior accepting her diploma.

Matt grinned down at her. "Matt. Remember? We're Matt and Cara. Right?"

"Right. Matt and Cara."

"You think I'm arrogant."

"And you think I'm a sassbox."

"Maybe we should start all over in our relationship," Matt said, again cupping his hand around her elbow.

Cara eased from his touch more reluctantly than she cared to admit to herself. "I wasn't aware that we had a relationship."

"You know what I mean. Our business relationship." Matt sighed deeply. "When I contacted Estelle about this job, I planned to work with Estelle personally. I'm not used to working with *underlings.*"

"That doesn't surprise me. But I assure you I won't do anything to this lovely old home that doesn't have Estelle's approval. And yours."

For a moment Matt stared at Cara, his gaze again roving over her figure, pausing at the V neckline of her white robe, her waistline, her hips, her trim ankles. Again Cara stood straighter, trying to control the depth of the neckline yet suspecting that her stance was merely making her bustline appear more prominent.

"Perhaps we'll get along all right, Cara. Since I'm financing this overhaul, I'll have the last say as to what will be done. Of course I'll listen to your advice and to Estelle's."

"That's comforting."

"There you go being sarcastic again."

"And I apologize again. Shall we get on with the tour? It's really growing late and you did mention that you had an appointment."

Cara walked up the stairs first. She was tempted to give her hips a slight suggestive swing just to reinforce her sassbox image, but she checked the impulse. Her own reputation and that of House of LaDeaux were at stake.

When they reached the second floor, Matt again took over as tour guide. "Of course you've seen the suite you're occupying, so let's look into this next one. There are three suites on the left of the hallway and three on the right. I want one suite decorated as a children's playroom-bedroom combination."

Cara hid her surprise. She hadn't imagined Matt and Jass with children. How many? Boys? Girls? Clearly, Matt intended for his children to feel at home at Grandma's house.

One by one they entered the musty-smelling suites, but now Matt was hurrying her through so quickly that when they finished the tour the whole second floor was merely a blur of blackened fire-places, crumbling mantels and faded wallpaper. And she was to be responsible for healing the decay that had taken its toll over nearly a century? In that moment the task seemed overwhelming. Is this what Matt had intended? Was he trying to make her feel inadequate and incapable?

"Where does this stairway lead?" She paused with her hand on the brass doorknob of a closed door.

"That opens into the stairwell to my third floor office. We needn't go up today. I don't believe Mother will be entertaining to the extent that the ballroom will become an immediate necessity. But of course, I do want it redone in a proper manner."

Cara headed for her own suite and stood with her back to the door. "Thank you for showing me through the house, Matt. I'm looking forward to supervising this project."

"You're trying to get rid of me."

"Of course not, but we've seen the house, haven't we?"

"We haven't seen the verandas and the grounds. Do you have plans for the evening?"

"Yes," Cara said firmly. "I plan to rest, to wash my hair, to retire early."

"I wouldn't want to interfere with anything as important as that. But surely those chores can wait until you've viewed the grounds and what's left of the gardens."

"Of course." Again Cara descended the stairs ahead of Matt and stepped onto the front veranda.

"Notice the latticework gingerbread decorating this porch, Cara." Matt pointed to the lacy scrollwork design near the roof. "It took one carpenter five years of hand carving to complete these intricate patterns. They're like decorations on a wedding cake, they're so fancy."

"A coat of white paint will highlight this work nicely." Cara scuffed at the peeling gray paint clinging to the floor boards. "Why did they always paint porch floors gray?"

"You're the decorator. You tell me."

"I'm afraid I can't. But I'll do some research on the subject and let you know what I learn."

"I'd like to see porch floors that match the blue tile of the roof," Matt said. "Bear that in mind, okay?"

Matt stepped from the veranda, motioning Cara to follow as he eased along an uneven bricked path overtangled with coarse vines and low-growing scrub. At the side of the house they reached an area that had once been landscaped with a central wishing well surrounded by oleanders now spiking through the tangle of undergrowth. Cara smelled dank earth as they stirred leaves and branches that had not been intruded upon for years.

"Here's where the mansion got its name," Matt said. "Oleander House."

Cara touched a pink oleander blossom with her fingertip, leaning forward to smell its subtle fragrance. When she glanced back at Matt, she saw unmasked enthusiasm lighting his face.

"The first oleander plants were brought here from Jamaica in 1841 by a roving sea captain, Cara. He gave the plants to friends who in turn gave slips and cuttings to more friends until oleanders were spread all over the island. The former owner of this house nurtured sixty varieties of this plant into healthy blossoms. Many of them are still growing and thriving."

"You love oleanders, don't you?" Cara asked.

"I've done some experimenting with them myself. I'm trying to develop an apricot-colored blossom. It's fascinating work."

Cara watched Matt's face as he talked about the oleanders. Could a man who loved flowers be as arrogant as this man seemed? Suddenly Cara imagined Matt as he must have been as a child, a barefoot boy with frogs in his pockets and freckles on his nose and starshine in his eyes.

"Why are you smiling in such a wistful way?" Matt asked, again cupping his hand under Cara's elbow as he guided her back to the veranda.

Matt's voice had lost its harshness, now it had a mellow quality like a muted cello. He stood waiting for her answer, but she couldn't say she had been imagining him as a boy.

"You love oleanders too, don't you?" Matt asked at last. "You're imagining this romantic old place as it must have been years ago. This is what I had hoped for Cara, someone who would see this place as I see it."

Cara paused on the path, embarrassed that her thoughts were so much more personal than Matt had guessed. Before she could speak Matt leaned toward her and kissed her tenderly. His lips brushed hers as gently as velvety butterfly wings, making no demands, offering only sweetness. Cara closed her eyes, letting her lips linger against his until she felt her body responding to the kiss. Reluctantly she came to her senses and gently pushed Matt Daniels from her.

"Really, Mr. Daniels. This is a poor way for us to begin our relationship—our business relationship. It's not my habit to allow myself to be kissed by married men." Cara turned and flounced on toward the veranda, now feeling hot anger churning deep inside her. Surely that was anger making her knees tremble, making the very roots of her eyebrows feel hot.

"Hold on a minute." Matt grabbed her wrist. "What's this about 'married men'?"

Cara laughed bitterly. "Surely you haven't forgotten Jass."

"Of course I haven't forgotten Jass. Jass Whitney. My secretary. How do you expect a man to forget his secretary?"

"Secretary?" Cara felt more heat rise to her neck, her face, her hairline. "But you said—I thought—"

Now Matt's eyes filled with laughter as he gazed at her searching for words.

"Matt? Are you out there Matt? If you don't hurry, we're going to be late for the Martins!"

Jass's voice! Cara would have recognized the throaty, sultry tones and that nervous, hacking cough anywhere.

Matt abruptly dropped Cara's wrist. "I have an appointment, Miss Logan. You'll excuse me, please?"

"Cara. Remember?" Now Cara made no effort to hide the sarcasm in her tone.

"Yes, of course, Cara. You'll excuse me, please?"

"Why certainly. I wouldn't want you to keep Jass waiting."

Matt started to say something, reconsidered and stomped off leaving Cara standing alone. So Matt wasn't married. Why did that knowledge give her such a special lift? His marital status was of no concern to her. She scowled.

But a children's suite. For whom? Was Matt really fixing Oleander House for his mother? Maybe the local gossips were onto something. But again, it didn't matter. It was none of her business for whom he was redecorating Oleander House.

She walked among the oleanders until she was sure Jass and Matt were gone. She wasn't up to meeting Jass Whitney yet. She no longer hated her, but she remembered that once she had. She didn't want Jass to see her in the jersey robe. She wanted to look her best when she encountered Jass.

Once Matt's jungle-green Porsche was out of sight Cara rushed inside, locked the door behind herself and hurried to her suite. She ran a tepid bath, pouring in a luxurious amount of bubble bath. She let her robe fall into a white nest on the tile floor as she lowered herself into the tub. Luxury. Pure luxury.

The pleasantly cool water lapping against her warm skin lulled her into a drowsiness that precluded thinking more about Matt Daniels. She felt sure Matt was not thinking about her. Jass had many ways of making certain of that. When she thought she could hold her eyes open no longer, she pulled herself dripping from the tub and wrapped her relaxed body in an almond-colored bath sheet that matched the fluff of rug she was standing on.

After patting herself dry she slipped into her

bedroom. Turning back the bedsheet, she stretched out, letting the soft breeze wafting through the window play across her body. She had turned on no lamp, and now in the twilight the corner streetlight shining through the linden leaves sent dappled shadows dancing on the bed, on her still-moist skin. She jumped when the telephone rang.

"What about dinner, Cara?" Estelle's voice flowed across the line demanding attention, action. Cara felt low on both.

"I'm going to beg off tonight, Estelle. I'm already in bed."

"You've eaten?"

"Not hungry. That wonderful lobster salad will tide me over until tomorrow. What I need right now is sleep."

"I'll pick you up for eleven o'clock brunch tomorrow," Estelle promised. "Peace."

Peace. Cara still heard the word echoing in her brain the next morning when Estelle arrived in the scarlet Mercedes. They ate a late brunch in an open-air cafe near the seawall, Estelle her usual tourist attraction for casual passersby. After they ate, Estelle whisked Cara around the island, touching now and then at favorite places Cara remembered from high school days.

After they had driven by Seawolf Park, out to Lafitte's Grove where legend said pirate Jean Lafitte had buried some of his plunder, Estelle slowed the car.

"Anywhere special you'd like to go, Cara? Let's get all the sightseeing done today and tomorrow so you can settle down to work on Monday with no nagging longings to distract you."

"Enough sightseeing, Estelle, but I have some questions. Why did you try to make me think Matt Daniels was an older man? I pictured him as an aging millionaire preparing to blow a fortune on a whim."

Estelle smoothed her hair and gazed out a window. "I really didn't think you'd meet Matt quite so soon. And I didn't say he was elderly. You jumped to that conclusion. As I recall that's sometimes an unfortunate habit of yours."

"But you knew that sooner or later I was going to meet him."

"Matt usually isn't around his Oleander House office on Fridays. I thought that if you moved in and spent the weekend, you'd be so attached to the old-world charm of the place and to the idea of redecorating it that you'd stick with the job no matter what."

"You think that for some reason I'd throw over this job because of Matt Daniels?"

"I guess I'm weighing our lives, Cara, and the scales tilt in your favor. You worked your way through school. Years ago when the going got tough, I quit."

"Things were different then," Cara said. "The depression. It wasn't easy for a woman to earn her own way."

"I said I wanted a career, but the first time a handsome man asked me to marry him, I abandoned my plans with hardly a second thought. It was only after Jean LaDeaux left me for a younger woman and I was forced to take charge of my own life that I really settled into the decorating business."

"And what does that have to do with me and Matt Daniels?"

"You're so determined to succeed I was afraid you'd run if you saw a situation that might tempt you to abandon your career."

"And you think Matt Daniels might be that temptation?" Cara laughed. "Don't worry about Matt Daniels tempting me. He's handsome and he's rich, but he isn't going to lure me from my goal."

Estelle squeezed Cara's hand. "I'm glad—relieved that you feel this way, Cara. You and Matt will be closely associated in the coming months. I was really concerned about how you would react to him."

"I'll manage, Estelle. So relax."

"I was foolish to judge your determination by my own. But the continuing good reputation of House of LaDeaux depends on the Oleander House commission, and in my present state of health I know I can't handle the project alone. But enough of business. Where would you like to go?"

"I'd thought of going to the beach. Do you ever go there? I'd love to have a suntan." Cara checked herself before she added "like Matt's." She had wanted a tan before she ever laid eyes on Matt Daniels. She wished he would stay out of her thoughts.

Estelle turned the Mercedes around and headed toward Oleander House. "I don't go to the beach anymore. I'll take you home and you can spend the rest of the afternoon as you please."

After Estelle let her out, Cara took her time walking to her suite. July in Galveston was no time for hurrying and even Oleander House with all its shaded grandeur felt hot and steamy. She slipped into a black bikini, then into a shell and a wraparound skirt. After packing lotion and a towel into a beach bag she strolled toward the beach.

When she arrived at the sandy strip, she wandered to a stand where a swarthy man with tamale-scented breath rented her an umbrella with blue and yellow stripes. She inhaled the mingled odors of popcorn, cotton candy and the salt breeze as she lugged the umbrella toward an empty spot near the waves. Squinting up at the sun, she could feel the hot sand gritting into her open sandals.

Propping the umbrella into the sand, she spread out the bath sheet and rubbed suntan oil onto her skin. She stretched out in the sun. She had forgotten how good it felt. She closed her eyes and drowsed, the pleasant warmth relaxing her body. Somewhere in the distance, she could hear children shouting and a dog barking. Jazz from a neighboring transistor was punctuated by the rhythmic slap of the waves. She felt at peace with the world.

"Fifteen minutes per side is enough for a first outing, Cara."

Snapping to a sitting position, Cara glared up at Matt Daniels towering above her in leather-colored swim trunks. He was looking down at her with an amused, proprietary air. Infuriating man! How long had he been there watching her snooze, his blue eyes scanning her body?

"I don't need a keeper, Mr. Daniels. What I do on my own time is my own business."

"Perhaps. But it could be my business if it causes you to miss work." Matt glanced at his watch. "You're overdone on the front."

Cara looked at her skin. Matt was right. She was decidedly pink.

"I have my car, Cara. Let me drive you home."

"But I'm not ready—"

"Yes you are. Come along. Don't be stubborn." Matt reached for her hand, pulling her to her feet.

Cara wanted to argue, but she bit back her words. It was a long walk home and Estelle would be angry if she couldn't work tomorrow due to sunburn. She slipped into her shell and skirt with Matt watching her every move.

"Too bad to cover such a nice view," he said when whe was dressed. He lowered the umbrella and returned it to the rental stand, then he walked with Cara to his car parked in the shade of a palm, and helped her in.

"Are you in a hurry to get home, Cara?"

What could she say? Clearly Matt knew she had planned to stay longer at the beach had he not appeared.

"Would you like to drive out to Tiki Island?"

"Is there some reason I should like that? Where is it?"

"It's that small man-made island to the right of the freeway just before you cross the causeway onto Galveston. Your aunt is thinking of buying a lot out there."

"Whatever for? I'd think keeping up two places would be a little much for her. She's supposed to take it easy. At least that's what the doctor said."

"I don't think she plans to keep up two places. North Deer Island is a bird sanctuary and it's quite close to Tiki. Estelle plans to buy a lot on Tiki and use it as a base for observing and photographing birds. It would be nice for picnicking too."

"I didn't know she was into birds." Cara laughed.

Matt headed toward the causeway. How different he seemed today. He seemed to have removed his arrogance along with his business suit. Cara flushed; she was overly conscious of Matt's bare chest with its virile growth of tawny hair, his muscular tanned thighs in the revealing shorts. She forced herself to keep her gaze on the scene outside the car window.

They reached Tiki Island. The sinking sun had turned the sky into a fiery backdrop for soaring seabirds diving for their suppers.

"This island is really barren," Cara remarked. "No wonder I didn't remember it. No trees. Not much vegetation."

"You'll have to remember that not too long ago all this land was dredged from the bay, dripping and salty. In time there'll be grass and palms or pines."

"I'll take the palms," Cara said. "They're more picturesque. Show me the property Estelle's considering."

Matt drove down a narrow blacktop. Sitting well back from the sandy shoulders of the road were high pilings that supported new beach houses overlooking the bay. Speedboats and sailboats bobbed on the greenish water moored to cleats set in the low seawall.

"Those beach houses look like fat cranes roosting for the night," Cara said. "I suppose people build on pilings for good reason."

"At the turn of the century a hurricane hit this area bringing in waves that washed fourteen feet above the land. So now people build on pilings that extend fifteen feet above the sea."

Matt slowed the Porsche. "I live in that beach house just up ahead, Cara. Would you—"

"No I wouldn't, Mr. Daniels. If you brought me

here on the pretext of seeing property that interests Estelle but thinking you could trick me—well, whatever you thought, you're wrong. Please take me home."

"I'm an excellent cook, Cara. I could make us—"

"I said I wanted to go home, Matt, and I meant it."

"You're angry with me."

"And why shouldn't I be? Take me home at once."

Tires squealed as Matt turned the Porsche and sped back toward Galveston. Neither of them spoke, but Cara's mind bristled with prickly thoughts. Arrogant. Spoiled. Conceited. Why did this man think she would to to his home the minute he smiled at her?

Matt stopped the Porsche in front of Oleander House and before Cara could gather her things he was at the door, opening it for her.

"You needn't see me to the door, Mr. Daniels."

"Matt. Maybe both of us need to cool down, Cara. This is a poor way to start our relationship— our business relationship. I apologize. I shouldn't have tricked you into going to Tiki."

"You're right. You shouldn't have."

Now Matt took her arm and led her to the veranda. "It won't happen again, Cara."

"I hope not." Cara pulled from his touch, her skin burning where his hand had been. But the burning sensation was due to the sunburn, wasn't it? She flounced into the house knowing she was lying to herself. There was a magnetism between herself and Matt that she was going to have to guard against.

Cara went straight to bed after Matt left her, but

she lay awake a long time remembering the look of him, his touch. . . .

She spent Sunday on the beach in the shade of an umbrella reading the book Estelle had given her. She half expected to see Matt, but he made no appearance. It bothered her to realize she was disappointed.

Chapter Three

On Monday Cara dressed in work slacks, shirt and sneakers and went to the first floor of Oleander House to study the formal parlor. This would be her starting place in the decorating job that lay before her. The parquet floor and the high patterned ceiling seemed to call for plain but elegant wall coverings. Silk? She pulled some faded wallpaper loose, almost choking on a cloud of dust that came loose with it.

Cara hurried back to her desk, called a local fabric supplier and made an appointment to see his line at three that afternoon. Then returning to the formal parlor with a flexible tape, she dropped to her hands and knees and began taking floor measurements. As she reached to extend the tape around a floor-to-ceiling window a wisp of movement caught her eye and she turned to face Jass. Immediately, Cara was conscious of her disheveled appearance. She wiped plaster dust onto her slacks as she stood.

Jass was wearing a mustard yellow skirt and blouse that set off her silky blond hair. Cara noticed that her figure was ample across the hips, but her spike-heeled sandals accented her legs to good advantage. The pale green cover on the *Vogue* magazine she carried matched her eyes, and Cara wondered if Jass had planned such a detail. She guessed that few things about Jass were unplanned.

"You needn't pretend you're pleased to see me," Jass said.

"I didn't intend to," Cara replied.

"Good." Jass coughed. "I'm glad we understand each other."

"And just what is it that we understand?" Cara eased her tape back into its case gazing directly into Jass's eyes. Long ago she had discovered that a direct gaze could mask insecurity.

Jass shrugged and rolled the *Vogue* into a cylinder. "Let's let bygones by bygones. I mean you're not going to let a high school incident affect your attitude toward me now, are you?"

"I certainly hadn't planned to," Cara replied coolly.

Jass began to smile and gradually the smile grew into a chuckle. "You really should have seen the look on Rick Mann's face that night, Cara. Priceless! He really had intended to keep his prom date with you. Give him credit for that. But when he came out to his car, corsage in hand, and saw me in the back seat wearing that topless go-go costume, it blew his mind. Literally."

"I'm sure it must have." Cara kept her voice steady, refusing to let Jass goad her into an angry outburst she would regret. Now she was holding the tape so tightly that she could feel it cutting into her palm.

Jass laughed again and arched her back in a way that accented her full breasts. "Rick was an innocent babe, Cara. He actually believed my story that some evil old man had given me too much wine to drink then abandoned me in the street and that I had crawled into Rick's car for refuge. From that moment on it was some night! You wouldn't believe! But all that's past and forgotten. I have a message for you."

"Then deliver it, please." Cara waited, forcing herself to be calm and businesslike. How could a sophisticated man of the world like Matt Daniels be taken in by a phony like Jass!

"The message is from Matt. He's picking you up at three o'clock today. He wants to take you to tour The Bishop's Palace to get you in the mood for working on this mangy hole."

Now Cara saw Jass through a shimmer of anger. How dare Jass deliver ultimatums! How dare Matt issue commands! "Will you please tell Mr. Daniels that I have a previous appointment?"

"I'll be absolutely delighted to deliver that message, Cara. Not that I'm going to worry about you and Matt being thrown together. You're really not his type at all, and I know you'll bear in mind that I saw him first. I could jinx this whole Oleander House project for you, you know."

Cara preferred to ignore the threat in Jass's voice. "My business with Mr. Daniels is purely on a professional basis. I represent House of LaDeaux and—"

"Oh, sure, sure." Jass shifted her gum from one

cheek to the other. "I saw you kiss Matt in the
garden last Friday. Very touching. A schoolgirl kiss
if I ever saw one." Jass laughed. "But I liked your
outfit. Nice try there. You'll grow up one of these
days, Cara. Just hang in there. But find someone
else to practice your wiles on. Matt's taken."

Cara fought to keep her hatred for Jass a remembered emotion only. And she tried not to imagine
the kisses Jass and Matt shared or the manner in
which Jass might deliver her favors. "Will you please
get my message to Mr. Daniels?"

"Yes, of course."

"Then I believe that's all we have to say to each
other right now, isn't it?"

Without answering, Jass turned and stalked from
the room. Cara listened to her footsteps on the
stairs, on the second floor hallway, on the steps
leading to the ballroom. Only when the sounds died
did she return to her office. She spent the first part of
the afternoon making appointments with furniture
dealers, paint dealers and carpet experts.

She was unpleasantly surprised when Matt strode
into her office and stood towering above her desk. "I
thought you would be dressed by now." Matt
glanced at his watch. "If we get there by three, you
should be able to see most of the outstanding
features. With me directing our tour we can avoid
unimportant trivia."

Cara felt her fingers tremble. "But I told you I had
another appointment at three o'clock today. It's
quite impossible for me to—"

"What do you mean!" Matt's blue eyes snapped.
"You told me? I told you—"

Cara interrupted. "Jass gave me your message this

morning and I asked her to tell you that I had a previous appointment. I assume she delivered my message."

Cara knew from the look on Matt's face that Jass had not delivered the message, and suddenly Jass's threat became a reality. She could jinx this whole project and Cara along with it.

"Jass is very efficient," Matt said. "I'm sure she must have delivered the message and that my warehouse girl must have neglected to get the word to me before I left The Strand. I'm sorry you're not ready to go out. I'll expect you to be more punctual in the future. Get dressed now, please."

"But what about my other appointment?" Cara sensed that she was losing the confrontation. Anger constricted her throat, leaving a copper-penny taste on the back of her tongue.

"Can't you cancel your appointment? Since I've made time to show you through The Bishop's Palace I expect you to take advantage of the opportunity. You'll get lots of ideas from touring that mansion."

Cara stood and headed for the telephone.

"Tell me whom to call and I'll break the appointment for you." Matt stepped between Cara and the telephone. "Go get dressed."

Cara jotted the number on a slip of paper and handed it to Matt, hating the feeling that Jass and Matt were maneuvering her. She looked down at her dirty slacks and gingham shirt. "I'll just be a minute changing."

Matt grinned. "How about the outfit you wore last Friday, Cara? I liked that one."

Cara flounced into her bedroom, closing the door gently although her inclination was to slam it. She slipped into the saffron-colored shirtwaist, eased an elastic band of the same color around her hair, then slung her purse over her shoulder.

"I'm ready," she said to Matt, returning to the office.

"Then let's be off." Matt studied her from head to toe and nodded approvingly. "Not as nice as the white, but it'll do."

Cara hurried down the steps and onto the veranda. The Porsche was parked at the curb. Matt held the door while she slipped onto the plush seat. As he walked around the car to the driver's side, Cara glanced back at Oleander House. A bit of movement caught her eye and as she looked up, she saw a flash of yellow disappear from a ballroom window that overlooked the street. So Jass had been watching.

On the way to The Bishop's Palace they passed Ashton Villa. Cara glanced at the Italian architecture. Her American history class had toured the mansion when they had studied the Civil War. The house had served as a meeting place of capitulation between Southern and Northern forces.

"We'll tour that place too," Matt said, "Just as soon as I can work it into my schedule. It's an antebellum home, but many aspects of the interior would be interesting to you."

"I've been inside it years ago," Cara said. "But of course I need to refresh my memory."

"I'm sure you do."

Matt didn't elaborate on his comment and Cara bristled momentarily then relaxed, trying to quash her antagonistic feelings toward Matt. She watched his strong hands gripping the steering wheel, his bronzed arms contrasting with the pristine white of his sport shirt. She caught herself imagining what it would be like to cuddle up to Matt as she was sure Jass often did.

"In the future I'll expect you to be ready promptly for any appointments we may have," Matt said.

"I intend to be." Mentally Cara moved farther away from Matt. "But today I—I did cancel our appointment, you know."

"If you're insinuating that Jass neglected to inform me, forget it. Jass is the most efficient secretary I've ever had."

"I'm sure she is."

Matt glanced sharply at Cara. "What are you insinuating? That she purposely forgot to inform me of the change in plans?"

Cara didn't reply. She realized that her silence was more eloquent than any words could have been. An angry flush rose from Matt's neck, turning his ears the color of ripe plums.

"Let's drop it," he said shortly.

They drove in uncomfortable silence for a few minutes.

"Here we are," Matt pulled the Porsche to the curb. His tone was cold. "As we tour, I want you to pay special attention to generalities—floor coverings, wall coverings, wood trim and finishes. And do notice window treatments. These are the areas that you'll first be concerned with at Oleander House. We can tour again for an overall view of furniture, paintings and the like."

"Of course." Cara slid from the car and gazed at the towering structure that dominated the corner lot. "It looks like a château on the Rhine, doesn't it?" In spite of herself, enthusiasm crept into her voice.

Matt glanced down at her quizzically. "How many châteaus on the Rhine have you seen, Cara?"

Cara heard the put-down in Matt's voice. "I've seen no châteaus in an on-the-spot observation. But I have seen pictures, movies and television specials featuring such romantic mansions."

Matt took a step toward The Bishop's Palace, but Cara held back, still studying the overall view. The afternoon sun filtering through oak branches cast long fingers of shadow against the four stories of gray sandstone. Pink and blue granite mosaic on the porch gave the palace color.

"Take special note of the roof, Cara. I may have a similar roof put on Oleander House. This one features Baltimore Spanish tile. And notice the figure of the winged horse topping that turret. There are several horses and they were hand-carved right here on the premises by master craftsmen hired by the builder."

"Do you intend to add turrets to Oleander House?"

"No. I like the gothic lines of the structure. I just think its roof could be a bit more eye-catching."

Matt linked his arm through Cara's as they ascended a flight of blue granite steps which led up to the entrance and into the grand hall. Cara wanted to pull away from Matt's touch, yet she couldn't. She found it pleasant to feel Matt's arm linked through hers. Her mind told her to pull away, but her body refused to obey. She found herself reliving their kiss in the garden, remembering the sweetness of Matt's lips against hers.

"Notice this grand hall," Matt said as they entered the palace. "It's quite similar to the central hall at Oleander House."

Cara snapped from her daydreaming at the businesslike tone of Matt's voice, yet she was still conscious of his arm against hers. An elderly withered-leaf of a man approached them, smiling.

"Would you and the missus like a guided tour, sir?"

"No thank you," Matt replied. "I've visited here many times and now I have special goals in mind which I want to point out to—the lady."

Cara wanted to look at Matt, but she didn't dare. How had he reacted to hearing her called the missus?

"Make yourselves at home, folks," the old man said. "Please observe our no-touch signs and please don't go beyond the velvet cords strung across some of the doorways."

Matt nodded and paid their admission fee. Cara stood for a moment gazing at the hand-carved main staircase. "Polished oak?" she asked, looking up at Matt.

"Right. You know more about wood than I thought you might. Of course oak is usually easy to identify with its wide grain."

Now Cara smelled the sweetish fragrance of incense and guessed that the caretakers had to use it to combat the musty odors that tended to cling to any unoccupied home in warm humid weather. Standing at the foot of the steps she enjoyed the touch of a cool draft against her cheeks. She studied the stained-glass windows on the first landing of the staircase. Sunlight flowed through a fan-shape of reds, yellows and blues in one window, and the other window featured a holy figure in a flowing robe the color of grape wine.

"Why do they call this The Bishop's Palace, Matt?"

"The home actually dates back to the early 1880s."

"That figures," Cara said. "That's the period when Galveston enjoyed its heyday as Texas' cultural and commercial center."

"The construction took seven years, and the materials came from all over the world. The owners were Colonel and Mrs. Walter Gresham. After the colonel died the home was sold to the Catholic Diocese of Galveston and they used it as a present for their bishop. It served as the Episcopal residence and Diocesan office until Bishop Byrne died in 1950. Hence, The Bishop's Palace."

Cara wished she had brought a pen to jot down points which she wanted to remember. The silver and onyx mantle. The cherubs painted above an ornate mirror. A built-in sideboard.

"Matt, do you happen to have a ball point?

"No." Matt tightened his grip on her arm. "And I hope you don't either. I want you to just look—look and remember. When a person takes notes, he tends to limit his vision. Important ideas will stick in your mind."

"I hope so."

"If you forget something, just relax with the thought that it wasn't really important anyway."

They toured the palace from top to bottom, taking leisurely strolls through the upper floors in spite of the five o'clock closing time. As they stood once again on the front steps to the palace Cara felt as if she had been jerked into a different world, a faster-paced world. It took her a moment to adjust to traffic sounds, to the wail of a distant siren.

"Well, what do you think?" Matt asked. "Get any ideas?"

"I liked the arches at the second floor level in the rotunda. Perhaps we could hire an artist to develop some plaster moldings similar to the ones there."

"Cherubs? I hardly think my mother would go for cherubs."

"There are many areas of design one could draw from. Patriotic. Mythology. American folklore. Of course, if you don't like the basic idea, we'll forget it."

"I'll keep the idea in mind." Again Matt took her arm and as they strolled to the Porsche she was aware of the sides of their bodies touching, and she sensed the same awareness in Matt. He exuded an animal magnetism that couldn't be denied, yet he handled it so subtly that there was no way she could openly object without seeming like a prude.

Cara said nothing more about decorating ideas. She was busy trying to keep her mind on what she had seen. The muted carpet tones. The tapestry wall hangings. The contrast of dark woods against cream-colored walls. She was so lost in her thoughts that it was several moments before she noticed Matt had passed the Sealy Street turn.

"Where are we going, Matt? I've seen enough for now."

"And so have I. But you do have to eat, don't you? I thought we might as well dine together unless, of course, you have other plans."

Cara hated Matt's high-handed manner and she wished she had the nerve to tell him that yes, she did have other plans. But she had never been good at lying. Even telling a white lie always made the back of her neck itch. Anyway, Matt would catch her in her lie. She had a feeling that he would check up on her.

"You *don't* have other plans, do you?" Matt asked.

"No. That is, not unless Estelle—"

"Forget Estelle for tonight. This is her bingo night."

"You're kidding! I can't imagine Estelle playing bingo."

"Ask her—tomorrow. Tonight we're going to live it up on The Strand."

"Isn't five o'clock a bit early for dinner?"

Matt glanced at his watch. "You're right at that. So we'll go for a drive." Matt turned onto Seawall Boulevard and drove along the beach where waves frothed like meringue against the caramel-colored sand. Soon they reached a secluded palm-shaded spot where he pulled the car to a sea-view lookout.

A white shrimpboat bobbed in the distance. Gulls hovered above the craft like flecks of pepper spilled from a shaker. Farther toward the horizon the sun slanted a fiery glow onto the undulating waves.

Cara squirmed. "I would really prefer to keep our meetings on a businesslike basis, Matt. Perhaps you should take me home."

"Are you afraid of me?" Matt looked directly at her, his blue-eyed gaze probing her face.

Cara eased toward the car door. "Of course I'm not afraid of you, it's just that—"

"Perhaps you're afraid of yourself—afraid of a normal womanly reaction to the sea, the sunset, a handsome man."

Cara straightened and eased even closer to the

door of the Porsche. "I'm not afraid of anything, Mr. Daniels."

"Matt," he corrected.

"I'm not afraid of anything, Matt. It's just that I want to keep our encounters on a professional level."

"What makes you think I brought you here for any other reason?" Matt asked. "It was your idea, you know. I was going to take you to a sidewalk cafe on The Strand where we could sit out in the open and discuss The Bishop's Palace decor. I had in mind a business dinner. But it's early and we can just as well talk business here—"

"Perhaps we should go immediately back to The Strand," Cara said, angry that Matt was insinuating she had hinted that they come to this secluded spot.

Matt started the car. "As you say, Cara. Your wish is my command. I'm sorry you're so flighty. This is the very reason I preferred working with a more mature woman like Estelle."

Cara felt angry tears sting behind her eyelids. Matt Daniels was deliberately trying to make a fool of her. And why was she letting him fluster her so? Why did she keep jumping to the conclusion that he was trying to develop something more than a business relationship between them? Cara remembered their kiss in the garden. Had Matt thought it a schoolgirl kiss?

Matt started to back the Porsche from the lookout, then he stopped and turned off the ignition. Cara felt like screaming and kicking, but she forced herself to sit calmly.

"I thought we were leaving, Matt."

"Just a minute." Matt gazed intently through the

windshield at the shore some distance below them. Cara listened to the surf lap against the sand. Her lips felt warm and dry and when she licked them she imagined she could taste salt from the misty air wafting through the open car windows.

A drift of fog was blowing in from the sea. The sun was no longer visible. It was as if a gray veil had dropped over the car. Its green color blended into the misty fog until Cara felt that she and Matt were lost in space, that they were the only two people in the world.

Cara was surprised when Matt opened the car door and got out. If he thought she was going to get out and stroll through the fog with him, he was badly mistaken.

"Be back in a minute, Cara," he called over his shoulder.

Cara watched him disappear like a phantom into the mist and she shivered at the sudden chill in the air. The day had grown so pewter dark that a gray gull wheeling through the fog at one side of the car looked white against the mist. What was Matt up to? He had left the keys in the ignition. She could leave if she wanted to.

As swiftly as the fog had drifted in, it vanished. Once again, the gulls were black specks against the blue sky. In the distance she saw Matt striding toward the car. When he slipped beneath the wheel, his eyes were aglow. She sensed excitement shimmering just below the smooth surface he usually presented to the world.

"I just saw a pied-billed grebe, Cara."

"Wonderful. I'm thrilled for you."

"That's sarcasm."

"What did you expect? You bring me to this desolate spot, then you abandon me and—"

"Pied-billed grebes aren't summer residents here, Cara. It's very unusual to sight one in this area in July."

Matt seemed so sincere that Cara relented. "I'm sorry I was sarcastic, Matt. And I'm glad you saw the grebe if it's important to you."

Matt swung the car from the lookout and headed back toward The Strand. When he reached a rough portion of the brick-paved street, he slowed the Porsche to a crawl. Cara loved the old iron-front buildings with their awning overhangs flat as breadboards and supported on slim round posts. The gaslight lamps were beginning to glow, and Cara could smell a medley of odors—seafood, salt air and diesel exhaust from a passing truck.

"There's my warehouse." Matt pointed at an ancient iron-front building with fourteen-foot cypress doors boasting elaborate Victorian detailing. "The renovation of my office will take months, but I think it'll be worth it. This area has been designated a National Historic Landmark District."

Cara looked at the sign above Matt's warehouse that read DANIELS BUILDING SUPPLY. "It's very impressive, Matt."

"I think so." Matt parked the Porsche near a corner and after they alighted he took Cara's arm to help her up the three steep steps from the street to the sidewalk. Cara felt dwarfed by the high overhead awnings and by the towering doorways leading into the buildings. But more than that she felt dwarfed by Matt Daniels. This time she really did want to pull away from his touch, but she refrained. She wouldn't give him the satisfaction of knowing his touch bothered her.

When they reached the Old Strand Emporium, Matt released her arm. "We'll eat here, Cara. You like po'boys, don't you?"

"Sounds delightful."

They sat on rustic pine benches at tables fashioned from huge iron-banded barrels. Matt ordered white wine and a selection of cheeses for them to nibble while they waited for their sandwiches. They relaxed as he played selections on the antique nickelodeon.

"What the place lacks in plush carpets and tux-clad head waiters it makes up for in picturesque detail," Matt said. "I find it old-world and charming."

"A perfect spot for a business dinner," Cara reminded him slyly. She sipped her wine and watched passersby. "I feel like one of the tourist attractions, Matt."

"And a very attractive attraction, I must say." Matt grinned at her. "I like being seen with beautiful ladies."

"Somehow that doesn't surprise me."

Matt laid his hand over Cara's on the table top. "As the saying goes, 'There's always room for one more.'"

"As the saying goes, 'I'll pass.'" Reluctantly Cara pulled her hand from under Matt's, noticing for the first time that the air had grown cooler. They ate their sandwiches, washing them down with the wine, then Cara settled back to begin the business discussion.

"What do you have in mind for the floors at Oleander House, Matt? I think the parquet floor in the central hall downstairs can be restored, but upstairs those pine boards with the wide cracks in between leave a lot to be desired."

"It's really too nice a night to discuss floorings, Cara."

"Then take me home and we'll continue our discussion in your office or mine during regular business hours tomorrow."

"You are hardhearted."

"Definitely."

Matt paid their bill then linked his arm through Cara's again. Instead of walking toward the car, he walked away from it. Cara's mind ordered her to protest, but again her body refused. Matt headed through narrow streets toward the seawall and she went along, enjoying the soft humid evening, enjoying the company of a handsome man, enjoying the feeling of being protected, pampered.

When they reached the seawall, they stood looking into the distance. The sea was like black ink, each wave tipping skyward, washed with starshine. The living-fish smell of the brine hung around them and Cara felt the onshore breeze pasting her dress to her body. Gazing at the vastness of the ocean made her feel small and insignificant.

"The moonlight brings out your beauty, Cara." Matt looked down at her as he gently squeezed her hand.

Immediately Cara felt her defenses rise. "That's an old, time-worn line, Mr. Daniels."

"Matt. The line may be time-worn, but it's true."

"I suppose you think few women can resist that compliment coming from man-about-town Matt Daniels." Cara pulled her hand from Matt's, unlinked her arm from his and turned to leave.

"It's a long walk home, Cara. A sassbox like you will really be sizzling before you reach Sealy Street."

"I'll manage." Cara had taken no more than three steps away from the seawall when Matt grabbed her wrist, spun her around to face him, then pulled her to him in a tight embrace. This time Cara felt no gentleness in his kiss. His lips were firm and hot and demanding and his left hand cradled her head in a way that prevented her from drawing away. She felt blood pulsing through her body with each beat of her heart and she felt sure Matt could feel it too.

Then suddenly she didn't care to pull away, to lose the touch of those warm, sweet lips. She responded to Matt's kiss, pressing the curves of her body into the hollows of his until he was the one who drew away breathless and shaken.

"I knew it," Matt said after a moment. "I knew you didn't have a floor-sample kit for a heart. Please forgive me for forcing myself on you, Cara. But I had to be sure you were human, that you had feelings. I don't want a robot advising me how to redecorate Oleander House."

Cara clenched her fists to keep from slapping Matt. She had to get along with this man. "Take me home, please, Matt. This non-robot has a lot of thinking to do."

"About that kiss?"

"About Oleander House, of course. My career is the most important thing in my life. Our trip to The Bishop's Palace today has been most beneficial. I'm sure you'll see the results of it when I complete my report of recommendations for the mansion. And you can relax, Mr. Daniels. In the future I promise to behave in a much more professional manner. Of course I'll expect the same sort of behavior from you."

Cara knew she was talking too much and too fast, and deep down she knew she was spouting lies, but Matt must never guess. From now on she would act just as coolly mature as Estelle, no matter how she felt inside.

Chapter Four

Cara strode two paces ahead of Matt all the way back to the Porsche and when they reached Oleander House, she jumped from the car before he had a chance to open the door for her. She knew she couldn't bear it if he touched her arm one more time.

"You needn't see me to my suite." Cara flung the words over her shoulder. "I can manage quite well on my own."

"I'm sure you can." Matt's words sounded like staccato notes as he jogged to overtake her. "But when I take a lady out, I see her safely home." Matt had his own key ready and there was nothing for Cara to do but listen to iron scrape against iron as he unlocked the door and snapped on the hallway light. The naked bulb suspended from a black cord gave off a hot glare that robbed Cara of her dignity, making her feel like a suspect in a police lineup.

"Thank you for a memorable afternoon and evening, Matt."

"You're welcome, I'm sure. I'll wait here at the foot of the stairs until you unlock the door to your suite."

"That won't be necessary." Cara mouthed the words, but she knew it was useless to protest. Matt would stubbornly wait. She was still at the bottom of the staircase when the telephone in her suite began ringing. She ran up the steps, key in hand. Surely Estelle was trying to reach her. Eight—nine—ten—Cara counted the rings, glad for an excuse to hurry away from Matt.

When she reached her door, she fumbled with the lock. Eleven—twelve—thirteen. The phone continued to ring. Now Matt was pounding up the stairs behind her.

"Better let me help."

"That won't be necessary. I have it unlocked now." Fourteen—fifteen—Cara entered her suite then slammed the door behind herself and grabbed for the telephone.

"Hello—hello—Cara Logan speaking—" The line hummed for a moment before Cara heard the click of a receiver. The dial tone buzzed in her ear.

For a moment Cara felt a chill feather across the nape of her neck, then she replaced the receiver in its cradle and walked on through her office into her bedroom. The caller must have been Estelle. She had probably been replacing her receiver on its hook when Cara answered. Naturally she wouldn't have heard Cara's voice. She would call Estelle as soon as she had relaxed for a few moments. No use to try to talk to anyone while she was still tense and keyed up from being with Matt.

Cara kicked off her shoes, realizing for the first time how cramped her feet were. An ache that she never noticed, unless overtired and tense, twinged along the back of her neck. She had just slipped from her dress when the telephone rang again. She took time to grab her robe before answering.

"Cara Logan speaking."

"Cara!" Estelle's voice boomed over the wire. "What on earth is going on over there? I was about to hop into my car and see if you were all right."

"What do you mean? Of course I'm all right. Matt just brought me home."

"Since when does The Bishop's Palace keep evening hours?" Estelle laughed in a way that made Cara want to explain but at the same time she resented explaining.

"Matt and I had dinner after our tour."

"Never mind," Estelle said. "I'm not prying into your private life. But I was concerned. I still am concerned. I tried to call you three times—on the hour, at that. And each time your line was *busy*. I'd wait a few minutes and try again, then nobody would answer. I can't imagine who could be using your telephone. You've got the only keys to your suite except the reserve keys I keep here at my place."

"I'm sure nobody's been in here, Estelle. I suppose if someone else were trying to call me at the same time you were trying to get the line, you'd get a busy signal. But why are you calling? Is there something I can do for you?"

"I wondered if you'd like to go birding tomorrow morning. I'm going to drive to Tiki Island for an hour or so."

"Estelle! I know nothing about birds. And you know I have to work in the morning."

"I'll get you back in time for a full day at Oleander House. Bird watching is an early-morning thing. Come on and keep me company. You might learn something. Anyway, I won't have you cooped up in Oleander House around the clock. That's one of the disadvantages of living where you work."

"What time does this birding adventure take place?" Cara stifled a yawn. But no. She couldn't use lack of sleep as an excuse. It was only a little after nine now.

"I'll pick you up around five A.M."

"Five A.M.! I didn't even know there *was* a five A.M."

"A change in routine will keep your mind sharp. Wear deck shoes and something earth colored. We want to be inconspicuous. Shall I give you a wake-up call?"

"You needn't bother. I'll set my alarm."

"Great! We'll come back to my place for breakfast. See you!"

Cara knew Estelle had hung up before Cara could change her mind. Bird watching! Five o'clock! What insanity.

Cara sighed as she finished preparing for bed. Once the light was off and she stretched out between the cool sheets she thought about the telephone. Then she thought about Matt. She tried to erase him from her mind but she failed. When she closed her eyes, she saw him leaning toward her and she remembered the insistent pressure of his lips against hers. She wondered how it would feel to lie next to Matt on cool sheets in the warm darkness. Reluctantly she forced her thoughts to other matters.

The telephone. Fifteen rings, but it wasn't her

aunt on the other end of the line. And if the line had been busy at seven, eight and nine, someone had tried to call her three times.

"It had to be Jass," Cara muttered. "Nobody but Estelle and Matt and Jass know I'm here except for maybe a few business people who certainly wouldn't be calling me at night."

Jass was checking up on me, Cara thought. When I answered, she learned what she wanted to know—the approximate time I came in. She did care that I was out with Matt. Cara turned her pillow over and closed her eyes, but it was a long time before she drifted off to sleep. What would Jass do to get even with her?

A little before five her alarm sounded. Cara groped for it, knocking the clock over with sleep-numbed fingers before she forced her eyes open, found the alarm lever and shut off the clanging. Deck shoes. She slipped into old sneakers then she found a pair of tan short-shorts, frayed and faded. But she had nothing but a bright yellow T-shirt to wear as a top. Did bright colors scare the birds? She grabbed a tan windbreaker.

Estelle parked at the curb at five o'clock sharp and Cara hurried downstairs. She hardly recognized Estelle without her makeup and she knew immediately something was wrong.

"What's the matter, Estelle? Are you ill?"

"It's nothing, Cara. I just don't feel up to this jaunt, but I want you to go. Will you do me a favor?"

"If I can. But I don't know anything about birds."

"You don't need to. I just need some color transparencies of wading shore birds. Any kind. I'll use them to design a mural in a home I'm working on. Here. Take this camera. Then drive me home and I'll go back to bed."

"Five o'clock! This is madness, Estelle. The doctor said you should take it easy."

"Don't lecture me, okay? Just take me home then get the pictures I need. They are really important to the Miller account."

"I'll try." Cara drove Estelle to her apartment then she headed toward Tiki Island, parking near the sandy lane that ran by Estelle's chosen lot. Wading shore birds. What if there weren't any? But there were. She could see them even from a distance. She felt dew on the ground cover of sea oats soak her sneakers as she spread a blanket out near the planked bulkhead.

"I'll just wait quietly and see if the birds will come closer," she muttered, studying the camera and sighting through the finder.

The predawn air felt cool and moist against Cara's cheeks, but the army surplus blanket scratched, and she sat on her windbreaker to protect her legs. In the distance she saw flames rising from the gas flares at the oil refineries. Somewhere she heard a dog barking and she smelled the scent of jasmine drifting from someone's patio. Certainly nothing as elegant as jasmine grew on this lot.

Cara watched the sky change from slate gray to a light smoky gray, to pale bisque, then shafts of pink light began to fan above her horizon. She couldn't remember the last time she had watched the quiet drama of a sunrise.

"You're up early."

Cara jumped when she heard Matt's voice. He had arrived so silently in a sailboat that she hadn't heard his approach. Matt wore jeans and a blue tank top that showed lots of tawny-colored hair in its U-shaped neckline. The outfit gave him a macho, outdoorsy look.

"I'm here on an errand for Estelle," Cara said. "She needs some shots of wading birds."

"Would you like to skim nearer to the bird sanctuary with me?" Matt asked.

"I thought bird sanctuaries were off limits." Cara sat unmoving although she knew Estelle would have grabbed the chance for a water to shore shot.

"You can't go onto the island," Matt said. "But we could ease close enough to watch the activity there."

Cara wanted to protest, but she knew she was trapped. Estelle had given her an assignment and now Matt was giving her a unique chance to fulfill that assignment. She folded her blanket and Matt reached for it. "I'll toss it here in the boat. Bring your camera and come on."

Matt offered Cara a hand. For a moment she hesitated, hoping for a way to board the sailboat without aid, but there was no way. The tide was out and the craft nudged the boards of the bulkhead several feet below the land. Reluctantly she sat down on the top edge of the bulkhead then clung to Matt's strong hand to support herself as she eased into the bow of the boat. She felt her pulse throbbing in her fingertips until Matt released her. He winked at her then, letting his gaze linger on her long legs, traveling slowly from thigh to ankle. Cara tried to ignore his gaze.

"So you're an early-morning bird watcher," Cara said as Matt pointed the boat toward the bird island.

"For some reason I couldn't sleep, so I decided to use the wakeful time to good advantage."

As Matt said "couldn't sleep," Cara looked away quickly. She sat straight and peered through her glasses on the pretext of looking for wading birds.

"We're in luck!" Matt leaned forward, listening. "Hear all the commotion? I want you to see a great blue heron before we go in."

Cara heard low-pitched croaks mingled with higher squawks and a shrill metallic screaming. "Noisy, aren't they!"

"Look to your left Cara. There's a heron at ten o'clock. You know, like on a clock face—ten o'clock."

Cara looked. "All I see are gray stumps along the shoreline."

"Keep looking." Matt pulled the boat closer to the island and suddenly Cara saw one of the "stumps" take flight. For a moment she followed the heron with her eyes. The huge blue-gray bird flew away from them with a slow powerful beat of its wings. Its feet extended straight back far beyond its tail, but its long curved neck was pulled in close to its body.

"Fantastic," Cara said at last, suddenly aware that she had been holding her breath. She snapped some shots of three wading birds, then she looked at Matt. "You and Estelle might make a bird watcher out of me yet."

"One blue heron and you're hooked," Matt said. He glanced at his watch. "I hate to say it, but I've got to get back. How about joining me for breakfast —juice, sausage, scrambled eggs and toast?"

"Not today, Matt. I've got to get to work."

"I won't take no for an answer," Matt said.

"You're coming. I'm the one you're working for and I say you have time for breakfast. Besides, I'm thinking of putting the beach house up for sale. This might be your first and last chance to see it."

"And I suppose the world will stop spinning if I don't see it?"

"Who knows. It just might. Come on, Cara. I can understand your reluctance to come in last Saturday night, but there certainly isn't anything particularly romantic about sausage and eggs at dawn."

"Okay, Matt." Cara avoided commenting on Matt's statement. Almost anything and any time could seem romantic if it involved Matt.

Matt helped Cara from the boat at her favored lot, but this time Cara managed to hoist herself onto the bulkhead unaided even though she scraped the back of her legs on the rough planking. She walked the short distance to Estelle's car then drove to Matt's place, parking behind Matt's car in the carport under his house.

As soon as Matt had moored his boat in the narrow boatslip behind his house he welcomed Cara, letting her lead the way up the long flight of steps to a covered deck patio where brightly cushioned deck chairs were arranged to give their occupants an unobstructed view of the sea.

"Do sit down, Cara. Give me just a few moments in the kitchen then we'll eat out here on the deck."

"Right," Cara said. "I'm starved."

She sat down beside a huge philodendron plant flanked on either side by large pots of avocado and ivy. No matter which direction she looked, she saw water.

"Watch this," Matt said, stepping from the kitchen to the deck railing high above the boatslip and tossing a crust of bread toward the bay. Cara rose to watch. Before the bread hit the water a gull snatched it and flew along the shoreline with five other gulls in hot pursuit.

"Is there anything I can help you with in the kitchen?" Cara asked, smiling at the mini-drama Matt had created.

"Not a thing," Matt said. "Breakfast is going to be simple. Buffet style. Come on in and get it, then we'll bring our trays out here."

Cara followed Matt into the section of the beach house on their right. Here an elegant but simple living room appointed with cool rattan furniture and woven floor mats invited them to linger, but Matt allowed no stopping.

"Right out to the kitchen, please."

They passed through a large dining room simply decorated in teakwood and brass with bare parquet flooring, and then they stepped into a sunshine yellow kitchen where Matt had set the breakfast out on a snackbar. The mingled aromas of fried sausage and coffee made Cara realize how hungry she was. It also made her wonder how often Matt prepared breakfast for a female companion. Jass? He had fixed the meal with an ease that bespoke much practice.

Once back on the patio they ate in silence for a few moments. Cara was still wondering at Matt's interest in cooking when he spoke up, looking directly at her.

"What do you think of my house, Cara? Bearing in mind, of course, that the interior was done by House of LaDeaux."

"It's really lovely, Matt. It suits you perfectly. Who designed the floor plan?"

"I did." Matt beamed as he answered. "I like the idea of the bedrooms being separated from the hubbub of the living area by this covered patio. It's really a practical floor plan."

"I can imagine." Cara heard the sarcasm in her voice.

"May I show you the bedrooms before we go?" Now Matt stood, gathering up their trays. "I'll do kitchen detail later."

Again Cara felt trapped, yet she wanted to see the rest of the house—the bedrooms. She followed Matt into a hallway, suspecting that there was nothing he enjoyed more than showing ladies into sleeping quarters.

"There are four bedrooms," Matt said. "Of course there's only one bath for each two bedrooms, so guests have to share."

Cara wondered who had shared these facilities with Matt, then she was angry at her own curiosity. Why did this man arouse such questions in her mind? Again Matt had kept the decor simple. Cool tile covered the floors, and bedspreads and draperies were fashioned from colorful sheets. All emphasis was on the picture windows that overlooked the bay. Cara stood at one window gazing out across the water wondering at its vastness and her own smallness when Matt joined her. They stood in silence for several moments before Matt spoke.

"Whenever I look at the sea I feel very important, Cara."

Cara couldn't believe she had heard correctly. This supreme egotist could look at the sea and feel *important!* How could she ever work with such a man?

"What I mean is—all this water around me

and—'' Before Matt could finish someone knocked on the door.

"Matt? Are you here?"

Jass! Cara recognized the voice and flushed in anger and embarrassment as Matt opened the door.

"Good morning, Jass," Matt said. "What brings you out so early?"

Jass's eyes snapped sparks as she eyed Cara, then she glared at Matt. "Have you forgotten your early appointment with Mr. Baxter? I tried to call you but—'' Jass looked toward a phone and Cara almost gasped when she noticed the receiver off the hook. So Matt had planned for them to be uninterrupted.

"Sorry, Jass." Matt replaced the receiver.

"I did forget the appointment. I'll be right in. Go tell Mr. Baxter, will you? Cover for me, please."

Jass flounced from the house and Cara heard tires squeal as her car left the driveway.

"I didn't realize it was getting so late," Matt said. He strode through the house quickly closing windows before joining Cara who had stepped onto the patio.

"Cara, I'll follow you to Estelle's place. Leave her car for her and I'll drive you on to Oleander House."

"All right. I know Estelle will need her car. But aren't you going to change clothes?"

Matt shook his head. "Baxter is interested in me, not my clothes. I have a change at the warehouse for later."

"Thank you for the boat ride and the breakfast," Cara said stiffly. Mixed emotions churned inside her. She regretted that Jass had found them together. She was angry that Matt had taken the phone off the hook. But at the same time she regretted having to hurry back to town. How irritating that Matt Daniels could so upset her!

Cara pulled from the driveway first, and Matt followed her until she parked in Estelle's apartment slot. Once in the Porsche she watched the scenery, saying nothing until they reached Oleander House.

Matt braked the Porsche a bit too suddenly, and she looked up quickly to see a white Continental parked at the curb. Jass was standing by the open car door. Again Cara was conscious of her inappropriate clothes as she gazed at Jass waiting for them in her form-fitted sheath.

She opened the car door and slid out without waiting for Matt's help. Carrying her windbreaker over one arm, she tried to walk with dignity up to the front door, but she couldn't help overhearing Jass's words.

"Matt! How nice that you've arrived! Mr. Baxter has been waiting upstairs since eight o'clock."

"I'm sorry, Jass. I forgot. I didn't mean to put you on a spot." Matt tugged at the tail of his tank top shirt. "I'll apologize to Mr. Baxter immediately."

Cara heard Matt's car door slam. She couldn't resist looking over her shoulder and caught Jass's angry glare. Jass's eyes had narrowed to cold emerald slits and Cara was sure that they had missed no detail of her impromptu beach outfit. And what was even more humiliating, Cara could read in that contemptuous, green glance the conviction that Cara had spent the night with Matt.

Chapter Five

Cara hurried inside Oleander House, and once in her own suite, locked the door. She wasn't ready to face the business world just yet. She heard Jass's step on the stairs. She held her breath for a moment as the steps stopped outside her office door. She wasn't up to facing Jass just yet either. Not in these clothes. Not . . . But she needn't have worried. She heard Jass walk on. Cara shuddered, wondering what Jass would do to get even with what she must consider an affront to her relationship with Matt. If only she could explain. But no. She owed nobody any explanations, especially not Jass.

She ran tepid water into the tub, bathed, then slipped on fresh slacks and a red and white gingham shirt. No use to dress up for the jobs that lay ahead of her today. She closed the door to her bedroom and opened her office.

"Cara!" Matt greeted her with a hand raised to

knock on the door. "My morning appointment was a quickie so I decided to come over here and see what your plans are for the rest of the day."

Cara quickly assumed a business-like air. "Fine, Matt, I need your advice. I'm just ready to go to the first floor to check out a few details. That staircase for instance. What kind of wood do you think is hiding under all that paint?" Cara picked up a small can of paint remover and a rag, then grabbed a letter opener along with a notepad and pencil.

"I feel sure the staircase is either walnut or oak," Matt said. "Probably walnut. It's wise of you to find out for sure before you go ahead with any more plans."

"I hope it's walnut. And I hope the ceiling and floor moldings and the door and window trim match the staircase. I can imagine creamy walls in either a textured paper or a textured paint as a backdrop for all that polished walnut, can't you?"

"That would be impressive," Matt agreed.

"And we could use a wide Oriental runner on the hallway floor in colors that would coordinate with the walls and floor coverings in the parlors and dining room."

When they reached the bottom of the staircase, Cara looked for a place where the paint had worn thin, then she applied the remover, rubbing until her fingers were numb and perspiration dampened her forehead under her thick bangs.

"Whew!" Matt made a face at the pungent odor of the paint remover. "We need some fans in here if you're going to be working with that stuff."

"Look!" Cara pointed to an oval patch of bare wood. "I do believe it's walnut. What do you think?"

Matt peered at the exposed grain. "Right. It's walnut. How could anyone bear to slap paint on such fine wood! You'll have to hire workmen to remove the paint—after you have Estelle's approval, of course. And of course, you'll need to get estimates for the work, contracts in writing and all that. I don't want to be bothered with the details."

"You've made your position quite clear, Matt. And I'm not afraid of the work involved." Cara chipped at the paint on a doorframe with the letter opener until she removed enough of it to make applying the paint remover practical. "It matches! Matt. It matches! Whoever built this old place knew what he was doing. This entryway will be fabulous when it's redone."

Cara led the way into the formal parlor, studying the high patterned ceiling, the Steuben art glass chandeliers and the parquet floor. The bank of windows on the south made the room light and airy as a solarium.

"How do you picture this room, Matt?"

"I don't want to influence you. This is your project. What ideas do you have for it?"

"I like the ceiling. I'd like to repaint it in a rich creamy color that would complement the walls in the hallway. Then I'd like to cover the walls here in plain claret-colored silk, leave the floor bare and furnish the room in Victorian pieces upholstered in a claret and cream-colored fabric with a design that looks like a woodcut print."

"It sounds plausible, Cara. Now what about the rooms across the hallway, the smaller parlor and the dining room?"

"I'd like to carry out the same color scheme there, Matt, the claret and cream." They stepped across the hallway into the smaller rooms. "But in here I'd like to reverse the colors, hanging creamy silk fabric on the walls and picking up the claret tones in Oriental carpets and in wall hangings. That way the whole first floor would be color coordinated."

"I hope you're writing this all down. You'll need to present it to me in writing so there'll be no misunderstandings later."

"It's down in my head and I'll transfer it to paper when I go upstairs. But first I want to check the condition of these walls. How many coats of wallpaper do you think are on here?"

"At least five. Maybe more."

"I'll find a loose edge and we'll check for sure."

Cara slipped her letter opener under a seam at a lower corner of a strip of paper, loosened the corner and pulled. Matt sneezed and stepped back as dusty particles of dried paste hung in the air.

"Sorry about that. I'll go easier next time." Gently she pulled up strips of wallpaper, faded white on top, then a blue flower, then a plain pink, a tan. "Only four coats, Matt. We're in luck. And the plaster seems sound."

"You can't tell for sure from inspecting one little place like this. You won't really be sure of the condition of the plaster until workers have removed all of the wallpaper. Again you'll need estimates and work schedules."

"That's enough for now, Matt. I'm going to my office and make out a written report. Thank you for listening to me." Cara turned and left before Matt could object.

She spent the next couple of hours telephoning for estimates on paint and wallpaper removal. She skipped lunch, using the time for writing out the written report on her ideas and noting the cost estimates. She made three copies of the report, one for Matt, one for Estelle, and one for her own file.

She slipped into her black skirt and a sophisticated black and tan blouse along with high-heeled sandals before going to Matt's office. It irritated her that Jass had caught her looking her worst on several occasions. But this time was going to be different.

The office door was open and Cara walked in. The high-ceilinged ballroom dwarfed the business office it housed. Jass's desk and the file cabinets looked like toys. Hinged screens decorated with seascapes separated Jass's work area from Matt's work area and from an austere cubicle that Cara guessed was a visitor's waiting room. If Cara had been rating millionaires' offices on a scale of one to ten, she would have given this setup a zero.

Jass was filing her nails and reading a fashion magazine. Cara noticed that the magazine cover matched the blue outfit Jass was wearing. Jass missed few details. And now she was acting maddeningly aloof, not looking up until Cara stopped in front of her desk and cleared her throat.

Keep cool, Cara admonished herself. *Don't let her ruffle you.*

"Yes, Cara. What can I do to help you?" The cloying scent of jasmine perfume wafted toward Cara.

"I'd like to make an appointment with Matt to go over these plans and cost estimates for redecorating the first floor." Cara heard her voice echo hollowly off the bare walls.

"My, you do work fast, don't you?" Jass gave Cara a sidelong glance that injected a double meaning into her words.

Cara decided to let that one pass. She stood silently while Jass looked over an appointment calendar.

"How about day after tomorrow after lunch?" Jass asked sweetly.

Had Jass emphasized *after* lunch? "I meant an appointment *today,* Jass," she persisted. "Matt wants to get this decorating project underway immediately. There's nothing more I can do until I have his approval. He's asked for this written report."

"Day after tomorrow is his first free moment," Jass said. "I am afraid you will just have to wait. Leave your report with me. If Matt stops by later this afternoon when he gets back from Houston, I'll give it to him."

"I prefer to give the report to him personally. I didn't know he had gone to Houston."

"I supposed he had told you. And when he returns, his schedule is full."

"Then put me down for day after tomorrow if that's the earliest possible time."

"Two P.M. Okay?"

"Fine."

"You'll report here, then?" Jass nodded toward the desk on the other side of a dividing screen. "Matt meets all his clients up here."

"I'd prefer to meet him in my office," Cara said. "I may have some sample books down there that he'll want to look at." Without waiting for Jass's reply, Cara turned and left the ballroom, conscious of her heels clicking on the bare floor.

Day after tomorrow! Surely Jass was stalling, trying to make her look bad. Did she dare call Matt on The Strand? But what good would it do if he was in Houston? Maybe she should have left the report with Jass. She hesitated, then hurried on to her office. She wouldn't give Jass the satisfaction of reading the report before Matt did and possibly finding fault. Cara could imagine Jass suggesting her own changes as she and Matt enjoyed steak and wine in some out-of-the-way restaurant.

Cara had only been back in her office a few moments before Estelle appeared. "My but how elegant you look, Cara," she remarked. "What's the occasion?"

"I thought perhaps I'd visit some fabric shops a little later unless you have other plans for me." She lied, not wanting to admit to her aunt she had dressed up for Jass.

"I do." Estelle motioned toward the street. "My car's ready. I'm ready. And it looks as if you're ready too."

"Ready for what?"

"A trip into Houston. The invitations for our dinner dance have gone out. The date is set for a week from Friday. We must make arrangements to get you fitted for some clothes. I've called a designer and asked him to make up a wardrobe in size ten. It'll be ready in a basted stage tomorrow morning. You have to go in for a final fitting."

"You really work fast. But if the outfits are to be ready tomorrow, why are we going into the city this afternoon? We'll hit the rush hour traffic."

"Most of that traffic will be leaving Houston, not going in," Estelle pointed out. "And I want to be there so we can get an early start on party plans tomorrow. The designer will see you at eight. Mr. Gino. You've heard of him, haven't you?"

"Of course, Estelle, but the expense—"

"Don't think about it. We'll see Mr. Gino first

thing, then I have an appointment with the caterer at ten and an appointment with a booking agent at eleven."

"Booking agent? For what?"

"For the music. Just a small group. Piano, bass and drums. Pack an overnight case and let's be off."

"You've made hotel reservations for us?"

"We'll be staying in Matt's penthouse suite overnight." Estelle held up a keyring. "Just got the key from him. He's a dear to let me use his place when he isn't in residence."

"When did you get the key?"

"Why just a few minutes ago. I drove over to The Strand. Don't worry about it. I use his penthouse quite often when I'm in the city on business."

"But Jass just told me that Matt is in Houston today, that I couldn't have an appointment to go over my report with him until day after tomorrow."

"Well, sometimes Jass makes mistakes."

Cara decided not to argue.

Her aunt must have noticed her set expression as she added, "I do hope you and Jass are going to get along, Cara. Why not let bygones be bygones and trust her?"

"How can you suggest I trust someone who just lied to me?" she burst out. "Matt himself says Jass is a very efficient secretary. Surely an efficient secretary would know the whereabouts of her boss."

"Anyone can make a mistake. Did you leave your report?"

"No."

"Well, why not run it right up there before we leave? I'm sure Matt will check in here later today. He can read the report tonight and be thinking about it."

There was no graceful way Cara could refuse without seeming uncooperative. She picked the report up and hurried back to the ballroom. Fighting the urge to let Jass know she knew about her lie, Cara laid the sealed envelope on her desk.

"Please give this to Matt at your earliest opportunity."

"Of course, Cara. You can depend on me."

"I hope so, Jass. I really hope so. I don't suppose it's possible that Matt has returned from Houston yet?"

"No. No, he isn't back yet. You'd be the first person I'd let know if he were."

Cara turned and left, feeling Jass's smug smile on her back until she was out on the stairs. No doubt the lies were Jass's way of getting even for the night she thought Cara had spent with Matt. Cara sighed.

"Cara, I have a surprise for you," Estelle said as they got into the car and drove toward the causeway.

"What sort of a surprise?" Cara said warily. She had already had experience with Aunt Estelle's surprises. And if it involved Matt . . .

"You'll need a handsome escort for the party, won't you?"

Cara's voice was cool, "I hadn't really thought about it. I supposed the two of us would go together." She held her breath, hoping Estelle wasn't going to say that Matt would be her escort.

"Hank is coming."

"Hank?" Cara tried not to act stunned. She had seen her father only two or three times since the divorce. "How did you locate Hank? I mean—"

"Is it all right, Cara? First tell me that. I don't want to make you uncomfortable, but, after all, Hank is my brother and your father."

"It's all right." To Cara's surprise she realized that she meant her words. It was all right for Estelle to invite Hank. Though she felt he had given her mother a dirty deal, she still wanted to see him. She knew the divorce hadn't been entirely his fault. Maybe if her mom had just fixed herself up a bit—tried a little harder. "I've—I've really missed Hank all these years, Estelle," Cara said to her own surprise.

"Well, you know Hank. Don't get your heart set on anything but a one-night stand. I certainly know that brother of mine, but he's family and I keep in touch with him through his Chicago booking agent. He's acting with a dinner-theater group in Corpus next week. He wants to see you, Cara, and is flying in just for the party."

"Hank Rockford." Cara said the name aloud. "Do all actors change their names, Estelle?"

"Lots of them do. Hank's agent advised him to change his, said Rockford sounded stronger than Logan."

Cara was seeing her handsome father in her mind's eye. Rangy and tall. Muscled thighs and shoulders that set off his narrow waist and slim hips. Tawny hair. Blue eyes. Hank was a quicksilver person always slipping away when anyone tried to pin him down.

Hank had been only seventeen when Cara was born. Perhaps his early marriage contributed to his roving eye later on. Even from the start he had wanted her to call him Hank instead of Dad. Maybe he was never intended to be a family man, she thought sadly.

"Hank will lend glamour to the party, Cara. I'm glad you're willing to have him as your escort."

Cara was still thinking about seeing her dad after such a long time when she heard the siren. Peering into the rearview mirror she saw the police car.

"Pull over, Estelle. Don't you see those flashing red lights? That cop's after you."

"But he can't be. I'm not doing anything wrong."

The siren grew louder. Flashing lights reflected through the back windshield into the Mercedes. Estelle sighed in defeat. They were almost at the causeway, but she managed to turn into the parking lot of a small shopping center. She switched off the ignition and began searching in her purse for her driver's license.

"Estelle LaDeaux?" The policeman leaned to peer at her through the open car window.

"That's right. Is there a problem?"

"No problem, ma'am." The officer smiled. "I'm sorry if I've alarmed you, but I have a message for you."

"From whom?"

"From a Mr. Matt Daniels. Mr. Daniels wants you to wait here until he arrives. I'll radio headquarters and they'll telephone him, advising him of your location. Is this agreeable?"

"Yes. Of course. Tell Matt I'll wait."

The officer left, and Estelle looked at Cara. "Now what do you suppose is up?"

"Maybe he wants his penthouse key back," Cara said.

"No use speculating," Estelle said. "We'll just have to wait until he gets here."

They watched traffic whizzing by on the highway, keeping an eye out for Matt's green Porsche, but when he arrived he surprised them both. Through the rearview mirror Cara saw Jass driving her own

Chevette with Matt looking ill at ease in the passenger seat. When Cara turned to look at them, Jass looked away, avoiding eye contact.

Matt leaped from the car, slammed the door, and as Jass sped away, he strode purposefully toward the Mercedes.

Chapter Six

For a moment Matt's virile ranginess distracted Cara from wondering what he wanted. Calvin Klein must have had Matt in mind when he created the sand-colored suit Matt was wearing. Matt's bark-brown shirt almost matched his skin and the tan and brown silk tie gave a special flare to his whole outfit.

"Can you give a hitchhiker a lift?" Matt leaned to speak to Estelle through her open window. "My car's in the shop and I have a spur-of-the-moment meeting in Houston."

"Why, of course you can have a ride, Matt," Estelle said. "Perhaps you should just take my car and Cara and I'll stay here. We can go into the city another day."

"No need for that, Estelle. There's plenty of room for all of us at my suite. And, if you're returning tomorrow afternoon as you mentioned to me earlier, our schedules will mesh nicely."

"Then get in and let's go," Estelle said briskly.

"I'll drive you ladies if you'd like," Matt said.

"Don't pretend to be gallant." Estelle opened her door and stepped from her car. "You know you can't stand to ride with a woman driver. Chauvinist."

Cara started to suggest that Estelle take her place, but Matt opened the back door, and Estelle eased onto the rear seat.

Matt slid under the steering wheel. "You ladies sure my presence isn't going to inconvenience you?"

Cara said nothing, waiting for Estelle to murmur the polite words Matt wanted and expected to hear.

"It will really work out nicely, Matt," Estelle said. "Perhaps you and Cara will have time to review her plans and cost estimates for the first floor of Oleander House tonight after dinner. Did you bring Cara's report with you?"

"What report?"

"The one Cara left with Jass. Jass was to give it to you at the first opportunity."

Cara saw a flush seeping under Matt's tan. "I'm eager to see the cost estimates. With your permission I'll return to the office for the report. I'm sure my rush to stop your car before you left Galveston caused Jass to forget about it."

"Of course return for it if you have time," Estelle said smoothly. "We have nothing pressing scheduled for this evening."

Matt turned onto a service road, circled under the freeway and headed back toward Sealy Street. When he reached Oleander House, he parked the Mercedes around the corner from the entry.

"Be right back," he called over his shoulder.

But before Matt reached the front steps Jass appeared on the veranda, obviously leaving the office for the day although it was only a little after four o'clock.

"Matt," she called out in her low throaty voice. "How nice! You've changed your mind about going into Houston?" Jass hurried down the steps to meet Matt, showing a lot of leg through the deep slit in her narrow skirt. She linked her arm through his when he continued walking toward the house.

"I've returned for Cara's report on Oleander House." Matt nodded toward the Mercedes. "I forgot to pick it up before I left."

Jass glanced in the direction of Matt's nod, and Cara saw a trapped look cross Jass's face. Then she lowered her voice to whisper something to Matt. In moments Matt returned to the car.

"Jass is unfamiliar with the report you have in mind, Cara."

With anger giving her confidence, Cara stepped from the car, walked to the veranda steps and faced Jass. "We want the report I left on your desk just a few minutes ago, Jass."

"But you left no report, Cara. Don't you remember? You picked it up and took it with you."

Cara felt her right hand ball into a fist. Were they going to stand here shouting "did," "didn't," "did," "didn't" at each other like fussing schoolchildren?

"Let's go upstairs and take a look," Matt said. "This has been such a crazy day that I certainly can understand how a report could have been misplaced."

They trooped to the third floor, Matt opened the office door and they walked to Jass's desk, now cleared but for the telephone, the desk blotter and the in-out basket.

"There!" Jass exclaimed. "You can see there's no

report. It would be in my in-basket if Cara had left it."

Cara felt sure the report was in Jass's deep shoulder purse, but there was no way she could demand a search. Better to bow out gracefully. At least Estelle would know the truth this time. "I must have been mistaken, Jass. I'm sorry."

"I am too, Cara." Jass's smile was almost a smirk. "I do hope the report turns up safe and sound."

"It doesn't really matter," Cara said. "If the report isn't on my own desk, I have a carbon in my file." Cara headed for the stairs, then paused. "While I'm here I should mention that you can cancel my appointment with Matt for day after tomorrow, Jass."

"Day after tomorrow?" Matt asked. "You were going to wait that long to show me your report?"

Jass smiled at Cara with a look of wide-eyed wonder, then she gazed up at Matt through her long lashes. "I tried to get Cara to accept an early-morning appointment tomorrow, but she insisted that she never goes to work before nine o'clock."

"You are a liar, Jass Whitney." Cara blurted the words then wished she could yank them back. She was going to have to find a more effective way of dealing with Jass than name-calling and she hated herself for losing her dignity in front of Matt.

"Now, ladies," Matt said. "We've all had a long, hard day. I have to make a phone call, but Jass, you can run on. Take the rest of the afternoon off."

As you had every intention of doing anyway, Cara thought.

"And Cara, get the carbon of your report and meet me at the car. Let's be on our way to Houston as soon as we can."

Cara hurried to her office, grabbed the report from her file, and rushed on down to join Estelle.

"Everything okay?" Estelle asked.

"Everything's just rotten. That Jass is trying to undermine me, Estelle. Said I didn't leave the report. Lied to Matt about an appointment I tried to make."

"Cara!" Estelle leaned forward. "This is very unprofessional behavior on your part."

"But she lied to Matt. How can I cope with that?"

"A businesswoman has to learn to deal effectively with her client's secretary. If Jass lied, then of course she was in the wrong, but you'll have to cope with it some way, Cara. Matt isn't going to change secretaries for your benefit."

Cara was about to argue when Matt rejoined them. She was glad he said nothing about her angry outburst, but she felt sullen and frustrated, and prickly as a sea urchin. She would have to be on constant guard. She would not let Jass wreck her career or cause Estelle to regret hiring her. They rode all the way into Houston with only Estelle and Matt conversing.

A traffic jam delayed them for almost a half hour, and before they reached the heart of the city Matt turned onto a service road then stopped at a grocery store. "I'm going to treat you ladies to dinner tonight."

"You'll spoil us, already we are staying in your luxurious suite," Estelle said. "Do let me take us out for dinner."

"No way, Estelle. I'm going to broil rib eye steaks that'll make your mouth water. Rib eyes, a tossed salad, and champagne."

Estelle didn't protest again, and Cara couldn't decide if she was glad or sorry. She wasn't particularly pleased to have Matt preparing dinner for her, but on the other hand the long day was beginning to tell on them all. It would be a relief to relax and not to have to dress and go out.

When Matt returned to the car, he carried a bulging grocery bag which he set on the seat between himself and Cara, then he drove on to *The Executive* in downtown Houston.

Cara ducked her head and peered up at the skyscraper that towered above the surrounding buildings like a mighty protector. Lights glowed from many windows and here and there Cara caught glimpses of people sitting on their private balconies enjoying the evening air.

Matt flashed his identification at the security guard at the underground parking ramp, then he eased the Mercedes slowly through the gloomy maze until he reached his private parking slot. They took the elevator to the penthouse floor, following Matt to a polished mahogany door bearing the number 2000 and entered the Daniels suite.

Now Cara smelled the clean scent of leather which seemed to come from all around her. She felt her heels sink into the thick pile of white carpeting. White and Morocco leather were the two predominating colors. Even the beams in the cathedral ceiling were leather-covered and brass studded.

"You've done a wonderful job here, Estelle," Cara said. "The decor suits Matt perfectly."

"That's what you said about the beach house," Estelle reminded her, "yet the two places are quite different."

"It's because I have such a fascinating personality," Matt said smugly. "First, city suave, then outdoorsy and unspoiled. How perceptive of you, Cara, to notice!"

Infuriating man! He probably means it too, Cara thought. She wished that she could wipe that idiotic grin from his face. Fuming, she walked over to the sliding glass doors that opened onto the roof terrace. She gazed out at the harbor below, only vaguely listening to Matt and Estelle's conversation.

"It is a wonderful setting for you, Matt," Estelle was saying, "even if I do say so myself. But of course, I had no part in your selection of *The Executive* as your city home."

"That's something I have Dad to thank for," Matt replied, a somber note creeping into his voice. "He spotted *The Executive* right off as a special place to live. I like to forget the scandal and remember the good things. This suite is one of the good things."

"After a dozen years, everyone's forgotten the past, Matt," Estelle said gently.

Cara wondered idly what Matt and Estelle were talking about. Not that it really mattered. There was so much about Matt that she didn't understand that she supposed one more thing didn't matter. And she had long since given up on Aunt Estelle whose imperious ways she had never questioned, even as a child.

She rejoined them for an in-depth tour of the suite admiring, for Aunt Estelle's benefit, the nine foot ceilings, the woodburning fireplaces and the dainty bedrooms.

Matt set Estelle's bag in a room decorated in sea-foam green, then led Cara to a boudoir awash with pale pink and appointed with white French Provincial furniture.

"You two take your time freshening up, and I'll have dinner ready before you know it."

"Matt?" Estelle called. "No offense, but I'm really not hungry. If you don't mind, I'll retire so I'll be fresh and rested in the morning."

"Are you sure you're okay, Estelle?" Cara asked, concerned.

"I'm fine. Now you two enjoy your dinner." Estelle smiled and closed her door.

Matt sauntered to the kitchen and Cara looked thoughtfully at Estelle's closed door. In spite of her aunt's exuberance, Cara knew that she tired easily since her illness. She rarely went to the beach any more. The heavy makeup she affected was not only vanity, it often concealed lines of fatigue. She would have preferred Estelle's company at dinner so that she would not have to cope with Matt alone. But she did not like to press her. Also, she did not want to admit to her aunt her mixed emotions about Matt.

She straightened her shoulders. She would make sure this would be a business dinner.

Cara unpacked her limited wardrobe. But now that Matt was here her limited wardrobe seemed all wrong. Her robe. She flushed as she remembered their initial tour of Oleander House. She certainly would never again appear in Matt's presence in that robe.

The sliding glass doors of her boudoir faced onto the penthouse roof. Cara opened them, pulled the pink draperies aside and stepped onto the roof terrace where an arrangement of potted palms added a touch of greenery to the scene. In the distance lights had begun to flash on, looking like specks of bright confetti decorating the city.

Standing at the corner of the terrace she could see for miles—the Katy Freeway, the Houston Ship Channel, San Jacinto. Below her sounds of squealing brakes and taxi horns seemed distant and remote like sound effects from a television show. She stood watching for the evening star and feeling the soft humid breeze like chiffon against her cheeks, cool yet clinging.

When she had had a momentary fill of the rooftop scene, Cara peeked into Estelle's room. Estelle lay sleeping peacefully so Cara retreated to a boudoir chair in her room, pulled out the Oleander House report, and studied it carefully, hoping she would be able to answer in a professional manner the many questions Matt was certain to ask.

"Cara?" Matt called a few moments later. "Come and get it. Again, buffet. We'll eat on the terrace, okay?"

Cara was more than ready for the rib eyes and champagne, but when she reached the serving bar, she saw chilled wine, a steaming casserole and a tossed salad.

"Looks delicious." Cara smiled and said nothing about the absent steak or the champagne substitute.

"Dig in," Matt invited.

They filled their plates and carried them to a table on the terrace, then Matt returned for the wine and wine glasses.

"It's delicious, Matt," Cara said. "But what is it?"

"Eggplant casserole. One of my favorite recipes."

Cara sipped her wine without comment. The casserole was good, thanks to much onion and cheese, but a little of it went a long way, and the wine certainly lacked the sparkle of champagne.

"Eggplant casserole is a poor substitute for rib eye steak," Matt said, a sharp quality in his voice. "Isn't that what you're thinking?"

Cara didn't answer.

"Be truthful. That is what you're thinking, isn't it?"

"Well—," Cara said, "you did promise."

"Right you are." Matt pointed to the casserole. "I did this for a reason. I'm trying to make a point. When reality doesn't live up to a previous promise, someone is disappointed. Maybe not seriously, but the disappointment is real. Right?"

"Right," Cara agreed. "Now, suppose you get to this point you're trying to make."

"The point is that you've promised to redecorate Oleander House for me in a way that will bring back its turn-of-the-century splendor. I hope you aren't going to promise me rib eye and deliver eggplant."

"Matt, how dare you!" Cara's voice flared. "I hate your insinuations, your threat. If—"

"I'm not making any threats."

"Then what is all this about?" Cara demanded. "You have to make this point of yours. I don't—"

"You're a novice at this work," Matt said. "I guess I'm still not totally comfortable dealing with an underling. I'm not easy on myself and I don't expect you to be easy on yourself either."

Cara took a sip of wine to cool the angry words that threatened to spew forth. "As soon as you're finished eating, Matt, I'm quite ready to present my first floor report. I think you'll find that I have neither been easy on myself nor on your pocket-book."

"Touché," Matt said with a laugh. "Those who desire rib eye must be willing to pay rib eye prices. You know me well enough by now to know that quality not cost is what I'm after."

They ate Matt's strange meal in silence, and after they finished Matt said, "I'll set the dishes aside and my housekeeper will tend to them. I want to get on with our discussion."

They carried their dishes to the kitchen, then Matt led Cara to the leather couch in the living room, opened her report and began reading. Cara sat and waited, nervously running her fingers over the luxurious leather of the couch.

At last Matt looked up at her, and the flood of questions began. What quality silk in the formal parlor walls? Would the claret shade be preferable to burgundy? American Oriental carpets or imported? Should the Steuben chandeliers of the parlor be matched with similar chandeliers in the hallway?

Cara was glad she had done her homework well. Matt's questions showed a thorough understanding of the Victorian period, and she had either an answer or a practical suggestion for every matter he queried her about. When their discussion ended, Matt smiled at her.

"Good work, Cara. When you promise rib eye, you deliver rib eye. I feel we're off to an excellent start on this project." He reached out and covered Cara's hand with his own. "Let's not let anything spoil this excellent beginning."

"Anything like what?" Cara drew her hand away reluctantly, feeling her fingers tingle where Matt had touched them.

"Anything like—Jass. There's an antagonism between you two that I don't understand."

"I'm sure that Jass and I will get along just fine."

"Perhaps. And perhaps not. But in the future when you need to confer with me, telephone me at the warehouse. My girl there will page me. I'll leave her instructions to that effect."

Cara felt as if someone had just cut a steel band that had been binding her lungs. She could breathe again. And Matt liked her work. He wanted to hear from her personally. She could hardly wait to tell Estelle the good news.

"I'm delighted that you're pleased, Matt. Now, if that's all for tonight, I think I'll go to bed. It's been a long day."

"I'd like to escort you to some night spots," Matt said. "Allen's Landing. Miller Theatre. Or even just to the cocktail lounge here at *The Executive*. All work and no play . . ."

"All play and no sleep . . ." Cara countered pleasantly. For a moment Cara pictured herself doing the town with Matt. Dancing. Listening to music in some intimate cafe. Sipping wine in the moonlight. But why tantalize herself with something that could only lead nowhere? "Thank you, Matt. But Estelle and I have a big day ahead of us tomorrow. I'll say good night now."

"Let's step onto the terrace for a breath of air before you go to bed, Cara. The view is magnificent."

Cara allowed herself that privilege, joining Matt in the soft starlight. When the music started, Cara started.

"Do you like the Stratford Strings, Cara?" Matt reached toward a transistor on the table and turned the volume up. A string orchestra was playing a beguine. Matt nodded his head to the rhythm for a moment before taking Cara into his arms. He danced with her, holding her so closely that her cheek was pressed against his warm chest. She could hear his heart thumping. Was his pulse always that fast?

Cara lacked the willpower to resist the dance and she relaxed as the music, the soft night and their desire for each other molded their bodies together. Only when the music stopped did she force herself to pull from Matt's embrace. But before she could walk to the door Matt stepped in front of her. He pulled her toward him and kissed her, his lips parting over hers.

"Matt!" Cara pushed him away. "That's quite enough." Cara pulled herself from his arms and this time she hurried into the penthouse without looking back.

Cara paused at Estelle's doorway. She had wanted to share the outcome of the meeting with Matt, but she was so unnerved by his kiss that she couldn't face her aunt. She entered her room, closed the door and slipped from her clothes to enjoy the luxury of a long, warm bath in the pink, oval tub. Wrapping the velvet-cut bath sheet around her body she toweled herself dry, then secured the towel under her arms sarong fashion and stepped onto the roof terrace.

The whole suite was dark. She hadn't realized she had spent so long in the bath. After a few breaths of fresh air, she returned inside. She slipped the towel off and laid it across the chair. Groping her way to her bed she lay on top of the rose-scented sheet, enjoying the soft breeze flowing through the open window. Was Matt lying in a similar manner on his own bed? Cara shivered at the thought.

She lay across the bed staring at the ceiling until

she could bear inactivity no longer. Rising, she peered from her doorway. Nobody was about. She stepped onto the rooftop and stood beside the potted palms near the terrace railing. The air felt like satin against her body, caressing breasts, hips, thighs.

When the music started again, her first inclination was to streak back to her room, but she was too late for that. She heard footsteps on the far side of the palms. Peering through the fringy branches she saw moonlight silvering Matt's tanned body, covered only by a towel cinched around his slim waist.

If she had allowed Matt to show her the town, she might be in his arms right this minute. A chill prickled across her whole body. What was the matter with her? She had no interest in men, especially not in Matt Daniels—conceited, overbearing, arrogant as he was. Yet right at this moment Cara knew there was no place she would rather be than in Matt's arms. Her whole body ached with longing. If only she hadn't been in such a hurry to come inside a while earlier!

The music stopped. Cara held her breath. When Matt turned his back to her to look out across the city, Cara seized her chance. Noiselessly, she slipped across the moonlit terrace and into the comforting darkness of her room.

She pulled the rose-sprigged sheet up under her chin and lay listening to the music drifting from the roof terrace. Though the evening was warm, she shivered beneath the thin covering. What if Matt had seen her? What would he have thought? That she was trying to tempt him? Her face flamed. *Had she been trying to tempt him?* A part of her asked, but did not want to know the answer. She did not want to admit the obvious. That she was falling in love with Matt Daniels. It was a feeling that she had never had before and her body trembled with the knowledge of it.

She remembered Matt's tender kiss in the Oleander House garden, remembered the way the taut firmness of his body had burned through the thin fabric of her robe. She remembered his passionate kiss at the seawall. She was in love with Matt. Helplessly and hopelessly in love.

But Matt would never know her true feelings. Nor would Estelle. She would bury her feelings for Matt deep inside herself and forget them completely. And she would never allow herself to be alone with him except when business necessitated it. From now on she would concentrate on advancing her career. Cara turned over and after a long time she fell asleep.

The next morning Estelle prepared a breakfast of chilled guava juice and dry cereal. When Matt appeared, Estelle outlined her plans for the morning.

"Matt, Cara and I have an eight o'clock appointment with Mr. Gino at Fashion House, and I need a special favor from you."

"If I can oblige, I certainly will." Matt sipped steaming black coffee, waiting for Estelle to continue.

"I want you to come along with Cara and me. You have an eye for clothes. We'll be making decisions this morning about Cara's workaday wardrobe which we want to match her personality as well as the image of House of LaDeaux."

"Where do I come in?" Matt asked.

"We need your viewpoint on what looks good on a beautiful woman, Matt. Will you come along and give us your thoughts?"

Cara almost choked on her juice. Surely Estelle owed it to her to ask her opinion on having Matt join them.

"Perhaps Cara objects to such an arrangement?" Matt looked directly at Cara as if reading her thoughts.

"I'm sure Estelle and I need all the help we can get," Cara kept her voice casual, trying to please Estelle with her choice of words. But Cara felt as if a dogfight were taking place in her stomach. Part of her wanted to shout at Matt to stay away from Mr. Gino's yet another part of her wanted him to be there, wanted him to see her model the elegant outfits Estelle had ordered especially for her.

"Do come along," Estelle begged.

"I'll be glad to oblige if you really want my opinions," Matt said. "I have no appointment until ten o'clock. And I should be ready to return to Galveston by noon if you ladies have finished your business by then."

"After the fittings for Cara I have only to meet with the caterer and make final arrangements for the party refreshments, then I must call at Musicland Agency and make sure a trio is available to provide dance music." Estelle began clearing their breakfast things away.

"Let the mess go, Estelle," Matt said. "Loretta will be in later today. She'll straighten up."

Fashion House was just a block away from *The Executive,* so they decided to walk. Mr. Gino, dressed in a black business suit was waiting to greet

them at the door. Cara inhaled with pleasure the
faint scent of perfume as he ushered them into the
luxurious salon with its satin brocade wall coverings,
and teardrop crystal chandeliers. Her feet sank into
the burnt orange carpeting and she could see herself
approaching in the elaborate mirror facing her.

"We are delighted to serve you, Mrs. LaDeaux.
Please do us the honor of accompanying me to the
French Room. Everything is in readiness." The
wispy Mr. Gino seemed like a swaying weed com-
pared to Matt, but his voice was surprisingly rich and
mellow.

They followed Mr. Gino onto a silent escalator
that glided like a velvet ribbon to the second floor
French Room. Mr. Gino ushered them to a grouping
of French Provincial chairs upholstered in pastel
shades of watered silk.

As he clapped his hands sharply a model appeared
on the stage. She undulated across the stage with a
hips-forward, shoulders-back motion. Cara wondered if the girl ever dislocated her spine executing
such a maneuver. But she made herself concentrate
on the model's blue satin jumpsuit, sleeveless,
pegged at the ankle bone and snugged to the waistline with an ultra-suede belt.

The next model wore a pale gold sheath much like
Estelle's scarlet gowns. The skirt was slit to the thigh
and the bodice plunged in a deep V neckline. Cara
felt it would take a lot of poise to wear that dress
comfortably.

The third girl modeled a leaf-green caftan. Six
models appeared in all. When the modeling ended,
Mr. Gino spoke to Estelle.

"If Miss Logan is ready, she may now try on the

outfits and present them personally for your approval."

"Go ahead, Cara," Estelle said. "Slip into the outfits and let us decide how well they suit you."

Cara walked to the fitting room, conscious of Matt's eyes studying her departing figure. A lady in the fitting room helped Cara into the costumes, and she modeled each one on stage as soft calypso music played in the background. The garments clung to her figure in all the right places. Cara felt inner satisfaction at having Matt in her audience. She basked in his undivided attention, but after she completed her style show she surprised a frown on Matt's face.

"You're not pleased, Matt?" Estelle asked. "I thought each of the outfits was perfect for Cara. She needn't limit herself to one style gown as I have."

"I liked them all very much," Cara said, puzzled by Matt's frown.

Matt shook his head. "I'll give you my personal opinion, then you can do as you like. Do you have a car, Cara?"

"No, not yet. But of course I plan to buy one soon."

"Then for right now you may be using Estelle's Mercedes sometimes, right?"

"Of course," Estelle said. "Cara is welcome to the car if she needs it. What are you hinting at?"

"Two things strike me about this situation," Matt said. "Of course Cara looks great in all of Mr. Gino's creations. Each outfit is perfect for her, leaving just enough to the imagination." Matt let his gaze slowly rove over Cara's body before he continued. "But Estelle, I'm surprised you haven't thought through this thing more carefully."

"Thought through what?" Estelle leaned forward. "I've given this wardrobe careful consideration. Color. Fabric. Texture. Design."

Matt gazed at Cara again, studying her body as an artist might study a model. "Cara's a perfect moonlight and roses type, Estelle. I really don't see her in such sophisticated outfits. Moonlight and roses—pink. I'm surprised you didn't think of it yourself, Estelle."

Cara felt mixed emotions. It pleased her to have Matt consider her a moonlight and roses sort of person. But what about sassbox? That had pleased her too. Maybe Matt liked the opposite traits of her personality.

"Pink." Estelle said the word slowly as if hearing it for the first time in her life.

"Of course, pink," Matt said. "Why not have these six outfits made up in a warm shade of pink that will blend with your scarlet gowns as well as with the scarlet Mercedes? The two of you will complement each other when you appear together."

"How do you feel about it, Cara?" Estelle asked. "I think Matt has a valid suggestion."

"I've always liked pink," Cara said, "but you've already had all these outfits special-made for me. The expense—"

"It's tax deductible, Cara. Advertising. Let's not let monetary concerns cause us to choose a wardrobe that is less than perfect for you."

"Could they have pink gowns ready in time for the party?" Cara asked.

Mr. Gino stepped forward. "In all six costumes?"

Cara hesitated, but Matt spoke up. "Of course you'll want all six outfits for Cara, Estelle. You may even want to consider varying your own costume.

Not the color, of course, but I can certainly see you in the caftan or in the jumpsuit."

"Mr. Gino?" Estelle asked. "Can you do it? All six ready by Friday night so Cara will have a choice of what to wear?"

Mr. Gino smiled and bowed. "For you and House of LaDeaux anything is possible. Friday night. For such a charming lady as Miss Logan the work will be a pleasure."

"Then it's settled," Estelle said. "And thank you for your courtesy."

It was almost ten o'clock when they reached the street again. Estelle glanced at Cara. "Want to come along with me? You'll have a couple of hours to kill."

"If you don't mind, and don't need my help, I'd like to take a walking tour. Why don't I meet you at *The Executive* a little before noon?"

"Fine." Estelle turned to Matt. "That suits your schedule too, doesn't it?"

Matt nodded.

Estelle hailed the next cruising taxi, and Cara watched until she drove off, then she began strolling, looking at the banks, the shops, the towering business buildings. She walked for blocks and she thought mostly about Matt. He had Estelle wrapped around his finger. And Jass. And herself. How did he do it? Flattery. That was part of his charm.

Matt Daniels had a smooth line. He kept Jass at her best level of secretarial efficiency by wining and dining her now and then. Did he insure himself a spotless penthouse suite by flattering Loretta? She felt a rising anger. Now she guessed she knew why Matt had asked her out, why he had kissed her. He was merely trying to make sure he got good return on the money he was investing in the redecoration of Oleander House. How could she have fallen for such a man?

Cara returned to *The Executive* at the appointed time and the three of them drove back to Galveston. Matt went directly to The Strand warehouse; Estelle and Cara stopped at *The Emporium* for a Coke. They sat outside at a barrel table under the awning, sipping the cool drinks and watching the crowds go by.

Cara suddenly remembered the snatch of conversation she had overheard between Estelle and Matt the evening before. What *scandal* had Estelle said everyone would have forgotten in a dozen years? She decided to ask Estelle.

"Estelle, what was the big scandal that you and Matt were talking about last night? Something to do with his father? Is it a secret? Would you rather not talk about it?"

Estelle looked at Cara sharply. "Why do you ask?"

"No special reason. I'm just curious. I know he is redecorating Oleander House for his mother, but I've never heard him mention his father. Is he still alive?"

"There's no big secret about Jake Daniels' death, Cara. It was sad. It's still almost too painful for Matt to discuss. Matt's father started Daniels Building Supply many years ago."

"I knew Matt inherited the business."

"But I doubt that you know the circumstances of that inheritance. The elder Daniels made some unwise investments and the business started to go downhill. Matt was still in high school then. By the time he was graduated his father had become an alcoholic and the business was on the verge of bankruptcy. Matt's dad died in a sanatorium, leaving the debt-ridden business to his family."

"To Matt's mother?"

"To Matt and his mother," Estelle said. "Matt's mother knew nothing of the business world. She wanted to declare bankruptcy, but Matt refused to take such an easy way out. He wanted to go to college but that was out of the question so he started working in the business. He worked around the clock, learning things the hard way. And he took his lumps. Everyone thought he was fighting against insurmountable odds, but Matt surprised everyone."

"The hurricane shutters?"

"Right. He developed a new twist on an old idea, patented it and made a mint. In less than three years he paid off all his creditors and won the respect of everyone in Galveston."

Cara finished her Coke in silence. This certainly was not the story she had expected to hear. She had been hunting a wedge to place between them, but instead . . . She knew Estelle was speaking the truth. She had to admit to herself that Matt possessed admirable qualities in spite of the selfish way he used his charm to get what he wanted.

Chapter Seven

During the next few days party plans absorbed Estelle's attention, but Cara worked steadily creating ideas for redecorating Oleander House. She made second and third telephone calls in an effort to get cost estimates in hand. She worked out tentative color schemes for each of the second-floor bedroom suites. She sketched preliminary plans for the third-floor ballroom. The work seemed to progress more quickly now that she could contact Matt directly by calling the warehouse. She tried not to abuse the privilege no matter how badly she wanted to hear his voice.

On the Tuesday before Estelle's party Cara telephoned Matt on The Strand hoping to be able to finalize arrangements for the first-floor painting.

"What is it, Cara?" Matt's voice held an edge that warned Cara to be brief.

"I need a decision, Matt. Carson Paint has presented the lowest bid on painting the first floor. They're a thousand dollars under the next competitor."

"And who is the next bidder?"

"Ewers and Son." Cara read off the list of estimates for Matt's consideration.

"Let's go with Ewers and Son," Matt decided.

"But Carson offered you the best price."

"And sometimes Carson promises rib eye and delivers eggplant. Since it's my money I say let's go with Ewers."

"Certainly, Matt. I'll call Mr. Ewers today. I'm sure he'll be delighted. By the way, Estelle asked me to mention to you that she'll hire a crew to clean your penthouse after Friday's party. She doesn't want Loretta to have extra work."

"I'll tell Loretta." Matt laughed. "Estelle thinks of everything, doesn't she?"

"She appreciates your letting her use your suite, Matt. And so do I. It's very generous of you."

"The pleasure is all mine. I like to show off my toys once in a while, and Estelle has impeccable taste when it comes to entertaining. The party should be the event of the season. Now, if that's all that needs my attention at the moment . . ."

"That's all, Matt. Thank you for your quick decisions. I'll get back to these other firms right away."

Cara heard the click of Matt's receiver, then, before she could hang up, she heard a familiar hacking cough come over the wire. Jass? How could it be? Cara replaced the receiver gently, thought for a moment, then hurried to Matt's third-floor office.

She was unsure of herself, but she was determined not to show it.

"Jass, you eavesdropped on my telephone conversation just now, didn't you?" Cara heard her voice echo hollowly against the bare ballroom walls.

At first Jass just glanced up from filing her nails, giving Cara a look of wide-eyed innocence. "Whatever do you mean?"

"I heard your cough. You thought I had hung up, but I was making notes, still holding the receiver. Your phone here is connected to the warehouse phone, isn't it?"

"But of course, Cara. I'm Matt's secretary, remember? He's asked me to listen in on all his incoming calls, jot down subject matter and the name of the caller. It's very hard to keep our records straight with me here and Matt at the warehouse so much of the time." Jass tapped a black notebook. "I record all of Matt's calls, both incoming and outgoing."

"I see." Cara turned and left the office without another word. Surely Matt should have told her that Jass monitored his calls. Of course she'd not said anything of a personal nature to Matt, but she felt it was unfair not to have known their conversations weren't private.

Cara was so busy the rest of the week that she had no chance to mention the matter of the monitored telephone calls to Matt, but she sensed that Jass was worried about something. Had Jass lied about Matt's asking her to monitor the calls? She kept dropping in where Cara was working and planning, and for the first time since Cara arrived in Galveston, she seemed pleasant. It was late the afternoon of the party when Jass dropped her bombshell.

"I can hardly wait until tonight's gala, Cara. Aren't you excited?"

Cara didn't know whether to be disappointed or relieved. She had known Hank would escort her to the party, but she had been wondering for days if Matt would bring Jass. Now she knew. That was why Jass had been so friendly lately. She felt she could afford to be friendly since she had the top spot in Matt's affections.

"Well, aren't you excited?" Jass repeated her question. "The party is in your honor, isn't it?"

"Oh, yes. And I really am excited. It's just that I'm so busy here I really haven't had much time to think about tonight. I'm terrible at remembering names and I know I'll be meeting lots of new people, people important to Estelle—and to me."

"What are you going to wear?" Jass asked.

"I haven't decided yet what to wear, Jass. What are you wearing?"

"I have a new outfit that's a wow. Matt thinks it suits me perfectly. He has such excellent taste."

"I'm sure he does." Cara picked up her tape measure and her notebook, deciding she had endured all of Jass she could take for the moment, but just as she started to return to her office, Estelle arrived. Cara could tell by the down curve of Estelle's mouth that something was wrong.

"Problems, problems." Estelle dropped down onto a straight-backed chair and sighed.

"What is it, Estelle? Let me help. I think you're exhausting yourself with this party."

"Cara, something has happened to throw my plans off. First, you knew I decided to handle the flowers for the party myself, didn't you?"

"No, I didn't. When did you decide that?"

Estelle shrugged. "Oh, a day or so ago, I guess. It doesn't matter. Matt gave me the idea when he said you were a moonlight and roses type. There'll be lots of moonlight on that roof terrace, so I decided to use moonlight and roses as the party theme. And I decided it would be more convenient to work with a Galveston florist than to work with a florist in Houston."

"That sounds reasonable, but what went wrong?"

"Maybe I can help you," Jass said. "If there's an errand I can take care of, count on me. Matt's been in Houston all day and I'm driving in alone tonight."

Now Estelle looked at Jass for the first time. "Jass, maybe you could help out. I've ordered dozens of pink rosebuds which Cara and Loretta and I will tie to the terrace railing an hour or so before the party, but the American Beauty rosebuds which I'm using on the midnight buffet table won't be ready until the florist's closing time this evening. Cara and I should be leaving for Houston soon."

"Would you like for me to pick up the American Beauty buds and bring them with me?" Jass asked.

Cara hated to accept favors from Jass, but Estelle needed peace of mind. "Jass, your picking up the roses would be a lifesaver." Cara glanced at her watch. "I didn't realize it was so late, Estelle. Give me a minute to freshen up, then . . ."

"Fine, Cara. Mr. Gino has delivered a selection of gowns to Matt's penthouse. They're ready and waiting for us there, so just come along as you are. And, Jass, thank you for your help."

"You're welcome Estelle." Jass smiled at Cara strangely.

Estelle went with Cara to her suite while she

picked up her luggage. "Are you sure you trust Jass to get those roses there on time, Estelle?"

"Of course I trust her. You misjudge Jass, Cara. She's no longer the kid you knew in high school. She's grown up now. And as Matt's date for the evening I'm sure she'll do her best to make the party a success for his sake if not for ours."

"I suppose so." Cara hated the sinking sensation she felt every time she thought of Matt and Jass together. She was delighted that they were traveling to Houston in separate cars. Had Matt approved this arrangement?

The back seat of the Mercedes was overflowing with florist boxes when Cara slid onto the front seat beside Estelle. The fragrance of the rosebuds sharpened her feeling of anticipation for the evening. She looked forward to seeing her father. He was a party person. She knew he would be at his best tonight.

"Brief me again on some of the people I'll be meeting, Estelle. I'm going to try to remember names, but . . ."

"Relax. You'll do fine. Nobody will expect you to remember them all. Don't worry. Just have fun. All you have to do tonight is look beautiful."

"Well, at least tell me what you have planned for the evening?"

"First, I've asked Hank to get there a bit early. I know you two will want to talk privately for a few minutes."

"I'm not sure I'll know what to say to him after all this time." Cara twisted her fingers in her lap. "What does one say to a father who abandoned home and family and—"

"Don't be too harsh on Hank, Cara. He's an

actor, you know. Always traveling. Always on the move. And think how *he* must feel. The judge let you choose the parent you wanted to live with and you chose your mother. That did nothing for Hank's ego."

"If I had chosen to live with Hank, he would have run in the opposite direction as fast as he could go."

"Perhaps. Perhaps not. But try to forget past hurts and enjoy Hank for tonight, okay? He'll lend spark to the party and I'd like to see the two of you on friendly terms."

They were almost halfway to Houston when Matt passed them, honking and waving.

"If he gets picked up for speeding, we may not see him at the party," Estelle said, laughing.

"That's strange, Estelle. Jass said Matt was already in Houston. If his plans had changed at the last minute, surely Jass would have been in the car with him."

"You know how Jass is, Cara. She's probably cuddled so close to Matt that it just looked like one person behind the wheel."

"Matt was alone, Estelle."

"Then Jass is surely picking up the American Beauties as she promised to do." Estelle went on talking about the party, and Cara tried to forget Matt—and Jass. Jass slipped from her mind easily. Would Matt always occupy her thoughts like a shadowy phantom?

"After you've had a chance to visit with Hank, we'll get ready to greet guests as they arrive. Loretta will serve cocktails and snacks for the first hour while people are still arriving. Then I'll give you a formal introduction to the guests. After that a string group will play for dancing on the terrace. At midnight we'll serve the grand buffet. There may be a little more dancing before the gala winds down, each lady then leaving with a rosebud."

"Sounds like a perfect party," Cara agreed, admiring Estelle's ability to plan and manage such a function.

When they reached *The Executive,* Estelle presented an ID card to the security man and parked the Mercedes, and then they took an elevator to the penthouse suite. The two women slipped into their bedrooms to change for the party.

Cara had just put the finishing touches on her light makeup, when there was a tap on the door. "Someone here to see you, Cara," Estelle said softly.

Cara opened the door to find her father outside. For just a moment, they stood staring at each other. Even in that brief time, Cara could see the admiration in his eyes. She had forgotten how handsome he was—and, yes, she realized with a pang, she had been right, he did look like Matt.

They both had the same ranginess that set off their evening clothes, the same tawny hair, even the same cleft chin. Hank's hair had touches of silver at the temples that Matt's did not. Except for that they might have been the same age. But Cara wasn't fooled. Hank was an actor; he knew all the makeup tricks in the book. Even the silvered temples might be phony.

"Cara!" Hank took a step toward her, and Cara went into his arms. He kissed her gently, tenderly, then put his arm around her waist. She clung to him, unmindful of Matt and Estelle in the background.

"You two go where you can be alone," Estelle

said when they broke from their embrace. "Loretta and I will take care of the rosebuds on the terrace. Matt will help too, won't you Matt?"

Cara led the way to the pink boudoir.

"We have a lot to catch up on, don't we?" Hank asked, letting Cara enter the room first, then closing the door behind them.

Cara perched nervously on the edge of the bed, but Hank dropped onto a slipper chair.

"I've missed you, Cara. You probably won't believe that, but I have. Sometimes when I played a strange town, I'd pretend you were in the audience. You and your mother."

"Mom and I have missed you too, Hank. But we've been all through that. It's past. Not forgotten, just past."

"The present is all we have now, isn't it? But, tell me, Cara, what are your plans for the future?"

"Surely Estelle's told you. I plan to work for House of LaDeaux and to establish myself in my career."

"And who's your current boyfriend?"

"No boyfriend, Hank. That's the current no-no in my life."

"I suppose I've taught you that marriage and careers don't mesh well, haven't I?"

"I'm very proud of your career, Hank. Really I am. I'm proud to be your daughter. Neither you nor Mom could help that you were incompatible." Suddenly Cara realized her words were true and she felt more at ease with her father.

"Your mother?" Hank asked. "How's she doing? Is she happy?"

"She's doing okay. But who knows if she's happy?

She enjoys her job in Chicago. A receptionist in a doctor's office. It's pleasant work. She has friends. I think she's contented."

"Maybe contented is better than happy," Hank said. "But let's not get too philosophical. I came here to see you, to enjoy Estelle's party that will launch you into your career. Let's go meet the guests." Hank paused before the mirror, to smooth his hair and straighten his tie.

Cara watched him, a performer about to go on stage. Then she rose. Their meeting had been less painful than she had imagined it would be. Hank hadn't changed. Hank would never change. The world was his stage and he was always ready for the next act. She admired his confidence.

After Hank left the room Cara lingered for a moment before the dressing table. One tendril of hair needed to be secured. She opened the center drawer of the dressing table. As she reached for a bobby pin, a receipt from Neiman Marcus caught her eye. She could not restrain her curiosity. "One diamond solitaire," she read, trying to make out another word but it was smudged.

Cara banged the drawer shut. So Matt had purchased an engagement ring! Was it for Jass? Would they announce their engagement tonight? Shaken by her discovery, Cara returned to the living room.

Guests were arriving. Hank saw her and brought them both glasses of white wine. Estelle began the introductions. "Hank Rockford the famous actor— my niece, Cara—"

Cara's right hand was numb and her face frozen into a smile before she was able to slip onto the terrace and relax for a moment with Hank. The fragrance of roses wafted up around them, and with Hank's arm around her waist, Cara felt happier and more relaxed.

The musicians were taking their places on a dais set in one corner of the terrace.

"May I have the pleasure of this dance, Miss Logan?" Hank bowed and kissed Cara's hand.

"With pleasure, Mr. Rockford," Cara took Hank's arm, leaning forward to kiss him lightly on the cheek. "We'll dance till dawn."

As they walked toward the dance floor, she was conscious of Matt staring at her from a doorway, but before she had a chance to speak to him, Estelle advanced purposefully and seized her arm. "Come Cara, I want to introduce you to everybody." Hank followed as Estelle propelled Cara into the living room and called for attention.

"Ladies and gentlemen, friends all, I want you to meet my niece and my new business associate, Cara Logan. I'm depending on Cara to put new life into House of LaDeaux and I'd like to alert you all to her first project in Galveston—the redecorating of Oleander House for Mathewson Daniels. When you're in Galveston be our guest. Stop by and we'll give you a tour of Oleander House. And now I'll let Cara speak for herself."

For a moment Cara thought she would be unable to utter a word. Her mouth was dry and her hands felt cold. Then she caught Matt's eye, saw his sardonic smile, and knew she couldn't afford to let this moment defeat her. She cleared her throat.

"I think Estelle's said it all. I'm delighted to be working with my aunt and I hope you'll come to see Oleander House. It's a fabulous structure and I'm finding it fascinating to restore. I'm lucky to have Estelle's wisdom to guide me and I'm looking forward to a long partnership with her. Thank you all for being here tonight. And now enough talk. Let's get on with the party!"

Everyone applauded, then Hank took Cara's arm and led her to the terrace where the trio had started to play. Only one other couple stood in the dance area—Matt and a beautiful redhead. Cara clutched Hank's arm.

"What's the matter, baby? Speech get you down?"

"It's—that girl with Matt. Who is she? I thought Matt had invited Jass and—"

"You're leaving me behind, Cara. Jass? Who's she? And if you would like to know whom Matt is dancing with, let's go meet her. She looks like quite a dish."

Before Cara could protest, Hank was urging her across the floor to where Matt was.

"Cara, Hank," Matt began. "I'd like you to meet Lana Morton. We thought we'd help Estelle get the dancing started. Glad you've joined us."

"Pleased to know you, Lana," Hank said.

Cara nodded to Lana. "Nice to meet you." Cara was relieved when the musicians began playing. She eased into Hank's arms and they drifted across the floor. Lana Morton. Where had that girl come from? Where was Jass? A cold finger of worry began to prod Cara's brain. She tried to recall exactly what had been said back at Oleander House between her and Jass that afternoon.

Jass had never come right out and said she had a date with Matt tonight. She had implied that she had—hadn't she? Had something unexpected come up at the last minute that had kept Jass from being here? And what about the roses?

"That Lana's some dish," Hank held Cara farther away and smiled. "Matt really can pick 'em."

"So it seems."

"You're not jealous are you? Do I detect a green tinge in your eyes?"

Fortunately for Cara, a burst of music from the trio precluded any answer she might have made. Now other couples thronged to the terrace. Estelle's party was definitely a success. Everyone seemed to be having a grand time.

Hank bumped into more and more couples, murmuring "excuse me" as he went, then suddenly, Cara noticed they were dancing next to Matt and Lana. Hank released Cara and tapped Matt on the shoulder.

"Cutting in, fellow."

Matt looked startled, then he released Lana and stood staring at Cara. "Guess we're stuck with each other, Cara." Before Cara could answer Matt took her in his arms and they glided across the moonlit terrace.

"Hank seems like a nice fellow, Cara. You surprise me. I had no idea you preferred older men—and an actor at that. Known him long?"

Suddenly Cara realized Matt didn't know Hank was her father.

"I take it you've known Hank a long time," Matt continued, tugging at the subject like a dog worrying a bone.

"All my life, Matt. Do you mind if we rest awhile?"

"As you like." Skillfully Matt eased them to the

terrace rail and they stood in the shadow of the palms where Cara had stood on another night. Cara shivered. She knew she really should tell him Hank was her father, yet she hated to. Maybe if he continued to think Hank was her date, he would keep his distance in the future.

But before Cara could speak Matt nodded to the band. "The music's great, isn't it? Not too loud. Sexy and subtle. Of course, tonight there's no lovely lady spying on me from behind the greenery."

Cara felt heat rise from her toes and flood to her hairline. "You—you—"

Matt cupped Cara's chin in his hand, forcing her to meet his gaze. "Easy, girl. I really rather enjoyed being spied upon."

"But—but—you *knew* I was out here that night. You *knew?*"

"Of course I knew. Did you think you were invisible? I thought I handled the situation very tactfully under the circumstances." Now Matt was openly laughing as Cara jerked her chin free of his grip. "First time in my life I ever wished for a hurricane, a *palm tree-destroying* hurricane." Matt took Cara's hand twining his fingers through hers.

Cara started to pull away, but Matt stepped in front of her, blocking her way. He encircled her with his arms and he kissed her. His lips were warm and demanding and Cara felt herself melting. She was in love with this man. How much longer could she fight it? Matt kissed her temples, the pulse point in her throat. Then his lips sought hers again. Just as she started to comply with his unspoken demand, the pressure of his lips lessened and he was kissing her eyes, her cheeks, the V of her neckline.

As Matt's arms relaxed, Cara clasped her hands

around his neck, and pulled him closer, fitting her lips to his once more. She felt the flat leanness of his body through the thin silk of her gown. Now he was holding her more tightly, his hand caressing the hollow of her back where her narrow waist flared into full hips.

"Where would you like me to put the roses?" Jass asked, silently coming up behind them.

Matt's arms loosened as Cara spun around to face her.

"What are you doing here, Jass?" Matt demanded.

"Why, Cara invited me, didn't you, Cara?" Jass's throaty voice flowed smoothly into the night.

"I—a—you—" Cara spluttered, unable to speak.

"What is the matter, Cara? You and Estelle asked me to deliver the roses for you, didn't you? I've put them in the kitchen for the time being. You'll probably want to help Estelle arrange them while Matt and I finish this dance, won't you?"

Jass snuggled into Matt's arms, turning her back on Cara.

Chapter Eight

After Jass made her disruptive appearance the party seemed to last forever. Cara helped Estelle and Loretta arrange the rosebuds. Although the fragrance wafted around them, it didn't soften the vinegary expression on Estelle's face.

"How could this have happened?" Estelle muttered at last. "I thought that Matt had invited Jass to the party."

"Obviously that's exactly what Jass wanted us to believe." Cara couldn't help being a little glad that Estelle was seeing the true Jass. And she was more than a little glad that Matt hadn't invited Jass. But who was this Lana?

Estelle snorted and accidentally dropped a rosebud in the cheese dip.

"The whole thing's sort of funny in a way," Cara said. "Matt may be a smooth man about town, but I think he has some rough spots ahead of him—at least where Jass and Lana are concerned."

"And I think you've planned those rough spots, Miss Logan." Matt appeared at Cara's elbow, his face dark as a hurricane. Estelle hurried back to her guests, but Matt blocked Cara's exit. "In your zeal to seem hard-to-get you've overplayed your hand this time." Matt glared at Cara. "If I'd wanted Jass here, I would have invited her. Lana Morton is president of Morton Construction, Inc. You've caused Jass to insult a client."

"A client! I'll bet! Are you insinuating I planned this mix-up?"

"And just where did you get that slick gigolo who's posing as your date?" Matt glared at Cara again. "I'm sure the real Hank Rockford is far too busy with onstage activities to make party appearances. I've thought that ever since Estelle told me he was to be your escort. Who is that crude character you've hired?"

Cara drew herself up to her full height and glared at Matt. "Matt, if my aunt weren't the hostess of this party, I'd leave immediately."

"Perhaps that's exactly what you should do. I feel you've already imposed upon my hospitality."

Cara forced a smile and kept her voice low so that nobody would guess that a heated argument was taking place. "I'm really sorry, Mr. Daniels that Estelle accepted your offer to use your suite for this evening. But we can't do much about it at this point can we? And I will not allow you to spoil this party for me or for anyone else!"

Matt turned on his heel and stalked off.

"What in heaven's name have you two been fighting about, Cara?" asked Estelle suddenly appearing by the buffet table. "What a time to pick! Do you realize that we'll probably lose the Oleander House commission because of this? And it's all Jass's fault, I'd be willing to bet. Maybe you were right about her after all."

"I'm really sorry about this mess, Estelle. I'll apologize to Matt, if you think it will help."

"Enough time for apologies and explanations tomorrow. Let's get this buffet line started. Let's bring the party to a close as soon as possible. Smile, Cara. And keep smiling."

The party continued for another hour and a half. Lana slipped away unnoticed, but Jass hung around until the bitter end. Hank escorted Estelle and Cara to their car in the parking area and he was saying good night as Matt approached with Jass.

"It was a grand evening, Cara." Hank winked at her. "We'll keep in touch, right?"

"Right, Hank," Cara said, knowing they would not. She felt like crying, but again she chose to smile. "It was great seeing you."

Hank kissed Cara quickly, embraced Estelle, and left.

Matt stepped forward, clearing his throat. "Since you ladies are responsible for Jass being here this evening I'm sure you'll want to see her home. Good night."

Jass crawled into the back seat of the Mercedes like a scolded puppy and Estelle and Cara slipped into the front. They headed toward Galveston in silence.

"I suppose I should apologize," Jass said at last.

"Not a bad idea," Cara said.

"All right. Please accept my apology. I tricked you. I used you. But I'm sorry."

"Sorry because it didn't work out quite as you planned?" Cara asked. "Just what did you think was going to happen?"

"I thought Estelle had paired Matt up with *you* for the evening. Just for looks, you know. I should have known better when you didn't seem upset at knowing I intended to go to the party. I really hadn't planned to go, I just said it to annoy you."

"But when the deal over the roses came up, you just couldn't resist, could you?" Cara asked.

"I couldn't pass up the chance to see what was actually going on. I was beginning to believe that your interest in Matt was purely a business interest. I thought Matt would be glad to see me. You're really not his type, you know."

"Thank heaven for that," Cara muttered.

They rode the rest of the way to Galveston in silence. Cara watched the headlights stream a golden path onto the freeway, listened to the tires hum against the concrete, felt the lurch of the Mercedes as it hit small potholes along the way. Traffic was light, but even at three A.M. there were other cars out and about.

In Galveston they dropped Jass off at her apartment, then Estelle drove Cara to Oleander House.

"I hope you're not too tired from the party, Aunt Estelle," Cara said. "And thanks again for everything. I really enjoyed the evening in spite of everything."

"Me too, and don't worry about Matt and the Oleander House commission. These things have a way of sorting themselves out. And the party accomplished just what I hoped it would do. It introduced you to people who will be valuable to you—to us—in the business world. We'll just have to wait and see what happens about Matt and Oleander House. If we lose the commission, we've lost it, that's all. Now get a good night's sleep."

Estelle waited until Cara was safely inside Oleander House before she drove away. Cara let herself into her suite, locked the door and slipped from her clothes. She dropped into bed without even taking time to remove her makeup. For a moment before drifting off to sleep she relived Matt's kiss on the terrace and felt again the touch of his hand on the low hollow of her back. Then she closed her eyes and willed herself to sleep.

Cara spent a quiet weekend. She basked in the luxury of solitude, wondering at her capacity to sleep, waken, then sleep again. On Sunday afternoon she took a walking tour of Galveston using a tourist map which numbered picturesque homes and gave a brief history of them.

She passed the Chubb residence on Sealy Street, walking on, she studied the attached porch on the east side of Heidenheimer's Castle, then she strolled around to view the tower on the west side of the mansion. Both the porch and the tower had been added in a nineteenth century renovation of the place.

Cara studied the original slate roof on the League-Kempner home, wondering if Matt's idea of a new slate roof for Oleander House was sound thinking. She walked on and on. The Lasker residence. The Campbell home. The Grover-Chambers mansion. When her feet began to protest, Cara returned to Oleander House knowing her time had been well spent. She felt a growing respect for the turn-of-the-century architects whose creations in wood, brick and stone expressed the epitome of the taste and culture of their period.

On Monday morning Cara was barely up and dressed before a knock sounded on her office door. Matt? Her heart pounded. Mentally she had practiced for this first meeting following the party, imagining what he might say, imagining what she might respond. If only she could look at Matt objectively. But that was no longer possible. Once she had admitted to herself that she was in love with him, objectivity had vanished.

Cara opened the door with quiet dignity, but instead of Matt, Jass stood in the hallway. Today she wore a tangerine skirt and tailored blouse, but the scowl on her face belied the brightness of her costume.

"Good morning, Jass. What can I do for you?" Cara stood in the doorway, careful to give Jass no chance to enter.

Jass held a newspaper folded to the *About Town With Tanya* column. She tapped the newsprint with her forefinger. "Have you seen this?"

"No. I haven't read the paper yet. What is it?"

"Read it for yourself." Jass thrust the paper at Cara and sat down on the ebony couch. "Read it," she ordered. "It's all your fault."

Cara's eyes skimmed the page.

Man-about-town Mathewson Daniels surprised everyone at Estelle LaDeaux's posh party for her niece, Cara Logan, by appearing with two lovely ladies in tow. Only the ladies seemed to express displeasure at the situation. Perhaps it was due to Matt's obvious attentions to the lovely Miss Logan.

"Isn't that rotten?" Jass demanded when Cara looked up from the paper. "Can't someone sue a columnist for printing stuff like that? I think it's an invasion of privacy. I think—"

"Could I get you a cup of coffee, Jass?"

"I didn't come here to have coffee. I came to find out what you know about this article."

"What makes you think I know anything about it? You engineered your appearance at Estelle's party. I'm sorry if the results were a bit more than you expected."

"I'm going to sue!"

"Sue who? And for what? Your name isn't even mentioned in the article."

"But aren't you angry at having your name linked with Matt's? Maybe we could pool our money and hire a lawyer, and—"

Cara refused to dignify Jass's suggestion with an answer. After Jass had flounced out, she sat down at her desk and smiled. She didn't mind having her name linked with Matt's. Not in the least. Of course she knew Lana Morton was more than Matt's business associate just as Jass was more than his private secretary. Matt didn't fool her.

Cara was still smiling when Matt walked in without bothering to knock. It was the first time Cara had seen him dressed in work clothes—twill pants and a chambray shirt.

"I see you've survived the weekend," he said.

"Same to you. I suspect your survival was a bit more difficult than mine. Have you seen the paper?"

"I've seen it. And I'm furious."

"I'm sorry, Matt. Truly I am."

"Crocodile tears will get you nowhere."

"Okay, so they're crocodile tears. You can hardly expect me to cry real tears for a man who tries to deceive two women."

"And especially not for the man you'd secretly like for yourself, right?"

Cara felt her face blazing. "I won't let you use me, Matt. I'll not be another of Matt Daniels' girlfriends. You know there is absolutely nothing between us."

"I know no such thing. I remember that kiss behind the palms in the moonlight. No woman kisses like that unless she feels something for the man she is kissing."

"Perhaps it was just the mood of the evening." Cara tried to ignore the tingle in the hollow of her back. "Anyone can grow romantic with moonlight and wine and the scent of roses all around."

"Hank Rockford is your father, isn't he?"

Cara gasped.

"I was wrong about him being a paid gigolo. That's still another reason why I think you care for me, Cara. You deliberately let me think Hank was your date. You were playing your cards very carefully, knowing how some men go for the unattainable. The stage name worked out conveniently, didn't it? But your trick failed."

"How did you find out Hank is my father?"

"He showed me his I.D. before he left my place last Friday. Then I looked his name up in a theatrical *Who's Who*. Hank Rockford—born Hank Logan in Chicago. One daughter Cara."

For a moment Cara felt naked and exposed, then she realized Matt had gone to a lot of trouble to check into the identity of her date. The thought pleased her but she hid her pleasure. Matt must never guess her true feelings. And Matt must not withdraw from the Oleander House contract.

"Matt, I want to apologize about the party. Honestly, I had no idea that Jass wasn't your date for the evening. She talked about the party as if she had been invited. And Estelle had nothing to do with the mix-up either. She was genuinely concerned about getting the roses from Galveston to Houston. Jass volunteered to help and I accepted her offer. I hope you're not going to penalize Estelle for my error."

"Penalize? In what way do you think I might do that?"

"By asking Estelle to void the contract for Oleander House. It wouldn't be fair, Matt. Estelle is looking forward to having Oleander House among her credits."

For a moment Matt stared at her, then his eyes began to twinkle and the corners of his mouth began to quirk into a grin. "To void the contract would be absurd. I intend to hold Estelle and you to every line of that document. I like working with you, Cara. I like your kisses. I like your sassy ways. I do believe that by the end of six months I'll have you eating right from my hand."

Cara rose, stalked to the doorway and stood looking pointedly into the hallway. "If you have nothing more to say, Mr. Daniels, I have work to do."

"But I do have something more to say, Cara. Please be dressed for dinner at eight o'clock. I'll pick you up then."

"And what makes you think I'm having dinner with you?" Cara kept her voice cool, but she felt her heart pounding.

"Our contract convinces me you'll have dinner with me. It states that you promise to do your best to keep the decoration of Oleander House in line with its time. That means that you'll have dinner with me tonight at Sutton Place. It's a Victorian mansion converted into a restaurant. We'll study the decor over dinner. Eight o'clock."

Matt left Cara's office and she stared after him, speechless, unable to enforce her previous vow to limit their meetings to business hours. Then she dropped back down at her desk. At least Matt hadn't canceled the contract. She must phone Estelle with that news. She glanced at her watch. Too early for telephoning yet. Cara straightened as she prepared to continue her work on the second-floor bedroom suites. She could handle tonight's dinner. She would keep it so businesslike that Matt would be sorry he ever suggested it.

Cara spent the day measuring windows, prying under paint and wallpaper and matching drapery fabric to wallpaper samples. At seven o'clock she prepared for her dinner date with Matt, bathing, rubbing her body with rose-scented lotion and dressing in one of the pink silk creations he had selected for her.

"I'm nothing if not prompt," Matt said as he picked Cara up on the stroke of eight. "I'm pleased that you share my respect for punctuality."

Cara noted Matt's white suit, his brown shirt and shoes, and always the masculine scent of leather. She kept her voice calm in spite of the fluttering of her heart. "We have a lot to discuss. I wouldn't want to delay our work."

Matt drove to Sutton Place, a three story brick mansion decorated with ornate iron-trimmed balconies and pencil-slim windows. He parked in front of the mansion and they walked up the bricked sidewalk, opened the heavy iron gate that swung on noiseless hinges and entered by the front door.

"Mathewson Daniels," Matt said to the hostess who was wearing a nineties costume with an ankle-length full skirt, tight bodice and leg-o'-mutton sleeves.

"Yes, of course, Mr. Daniels. Follow me, please."

A scent of gardenia hung in the air though there were no gardenia blossoms in sight. Matt held Cara's chair for her, seating her at a secluded table in a small alcove. The hostess lit a pink candle inside the hurricane globe in the middle of their table, then left them alone. Care felt ill at ease because Matt had chosen such an intimate setting for their discussion, but she was determined to hold their talk to business matters.

"I hope you noticed the carpets, Cara," Matt said, as a waiter brought the wine list.

"What about them?"

Matt ordered white wine and waited until the waiter left before he answered. "I wanted you to notice how the decorator has used the claret-colored background of the carpets to unify the whole setting."

"I like it, Matt." Cara refrained from pointing out that the idea was quite similar to her plans for the first floor of Oleander House. "Is the rest of the mansion open for tours?"

"I don't believe so." The waiter arrived, first opening the wine and then presenting it to Matt for inspection. After Matt had approved it, the waiter filled two chilled glasses, placed the first in front of Cara and the second in front of Matt then left them alone. Cara enjoyed the dry coolness of her drink and waited for whatever was to come next.

"We must tour Ashton Villa before you go much farther with your second-floor plans, Cara. It's Italianate villa style, but the Gothic Revival detail is outstanding."

"Perhaps we could visit the villa tomorrow," Cara suggested, "I'd like to start getting estimates for the second-floor work sometime this week."

"Tomorrow's out." Matt poured second glasses of wine just as a waitress arrived to take their dinner order. Cara knew by the letdown feeling inside her that she had more than a casual business interest in touring Ashton Villa with Matt.

"We'll have the flounder stuffed with crabmeat filling," Matt said to the waitress.

Cara wanted to shout that she hated crabmeat, but she remained silent. How arrogant of Matt to think he could order perfectly for anyone and everyone. How she wished she hated crabmeat! Maybe she would just pick at her meal, let Matt know subtly that he made a poor choice for her.

"I would really prefer to tour Ashton Villa tomorrow," Cara said, refusing to let Matt organize her life completely.

Matt grinned and took another sip of wine. "That's up to you, of course, Cara. However, Ashton is closed on Tuesdays and you might find that a bit of an inconvenience. I had planned to take you on Wednesday if you can spare the time."

"Wednesday will be fine, thank you." Matt had a way of always winning that infuriated her.

Soon the waitress returned with their salads, then their dinners. The crabmeat filling was delicious and Cara forgot her perversity and ate every bite of it.

"I see you enjoy the finer things of life," Matt said, noting Cara's empty plate.

"It was delicious, Matt. You have excellent taste. But I'm sure you know that."

The waitress had arrived to take their dessert order and Matt had asked for baked Alaska when suddenly he changed his mind. Cara looked over her shoulder, following Matt's gaze. Jass and a tall football-lineman type were headed for the table in the alcove directly across from them.

"I believe we'll skip the dessert, Miss," Matt said.

The waitress had the check ready in seconds. Matt paid, then whisked Cara from the alcove, barely nodding to Jass and her escort. Cara knew from the thin white line below Matt's nose and above his lip that he was angry. Furious.

When they were in the Porsche, Matt spoke. "She's following me. She wants me to know she has other—friends."

"Perhaps it was just a coincidence, Matt. I really don't think Jass would do anything underhanded."

"Sarcasm will get you nowhere, Cara. We both know Jass. But I'm not going to let her spoil our evening."

"You mean our business discussion, don't you?"

"A business discussion can be a pleasure, can't it?"

"Of course." Cara tried to relax although she realized Matt was heading toward Tiki Island.

"We'll have dessert at my place."

"Fine. I suppose you baked a pie just this morning."

"Pastries aren't really my thing. I had in mind a bit of ice cream, a bit of crème de menthe."

When they reached the beach house, Matt escorted Cara up the steps and onto the patio deck, carefully refraining from touching her arm. "Outside or inside, Cara?"

"Let's sit outside. I love to hear the waves lapping against the boatslip."

Matt opened the sliding doors into the house and stepped inside as Cara relaxed in a cushioned deck chair. She had hardly settled herself before the telephone rang.

"Hello." Matt picked up the extension near the patio door. "Estelle! It's good to hear from you. Cara and I have just been enjoying a business dinner at Sutton Place. That's why you couldn't reach me."

Cara tried not to listen, and she sensed Matt lowering his voice, but even so snatches of the conversation reached her. And when Matt raised his voice in irritation, his words reached her quite clearly.

"I'm doing Oleander House to suit Gwen, Estelle. She hates bare floors. It's Gwen's preferences that matter to me, not . . ."

Gwen! For a moment Cara felt frozen to the deck chair. What a fool she had been to believe Matt's line. Had he fed Estelle a line too? Estelle had told her the gossip about Matt's redecorating the house for his ladyfriend. Clearly the talk hadn't been idle gossip at all. What were Matt's motives in this bit of subterfuge? Cara could only guess.

Maybe he enjoyed leading on his women friends, pretending he was redecorating Oleander House for his mother, then at the last moment bringing in the future Mrs. Mathewson Daniels. What a surprise for them all. Well! Fortunately, the overheard phone call had spared her this fate.

And there was no reason for her to stay here any

longer, now that she thought about it. She might have to work for Matt during office hours, but contract or no contract, she had no obligation to spend evenings with him while he made plans to bring his fiancée to Oleander House.

Cara got up from the deck chair and tiptoed toward the stairs just as Matt gave an irritatingly happy laugh into the phone. Let him save it and his ice cream and his crème de menthe and anything he cared to offer for Gwen! Cara would be out of the whole sorry mess.

Chapter Nine

Cara tiptoed across the covered deck then hurried down the steps as quickly as she could without making any noise to alert Matt to her departure. Gwen! She tried to picture a girl named Gwen. Blonde? Brunette? Redhead? No matter the color of her hair. Cara knew any girl who caught Matt's eye would be sexy and sophisticated and beautiful and confident and talented and . . . and . . . and all the other things she herself was not. She tried to hate Gwen. Could a person hate a person she had never known?

Following the lane leading away from Matt's beach house, Cara kept to the side of the blacktop until she reached the main road. A piece of broken shell lodged in her shoe forcing her to stop and remove it. She hated the delay. Matt mustn't find her along the roadside.

Distances were deceptive. Her feet ached long

before she came to the marina, but once she saw the familiar shed-like structure varnished with moonlight she forced herself to jog.

Water sounds on all sides masked the sound of an approaching car until it was almost even with her. Cara stepped far onto the shoulder of the road feeling her shoes sink into a loose mixture of sand and crushed shell. The car whizzed past leaving a slight trace of diesel exhaust. Had the driver been Matt? Would he come after her?

"There!" Cara spoke the word aloud as relief flooded through her. There ahead just around a curve in the road was a lighted phone booth. Although her breath already was coming in sharp gasps that made her throat ache, Cara forced herself to jog until she reached the coffin-like structure. She had entered the booth and closed the door behind herself before she realized how the overhead light spotlighted her. She stepped from the booth. If Matt should come hunting for her, she didn't want to be found.

Another car was approaching. She felt the vibrations through the floor of the booth. Matt? Quickly she darted through the opened door, slipped behind the booth and hunkered near the ground. What if Matt found her in such a ridiculous position? She could never explain her actions. She couldn't bear to admit that she was jealous of some woman named Gwen. How he would enjoy laughing at that!

What did Gwen look like? What sort of a personality did she have? Why did Matt's choice concern her? She mustn't let it. That's why she had left the beach house. She would get her own emotions under control. From now on all her Oleander House transactions with Matt would be held during daytime business hours. She had made that vow before, but this time she would keep it. What Matt did with his evenings would be none of her concern.

The car flashed around the curve and slowed. Cara imagined Matt peering toward the phone booth, seeing nobody, then speeding up again. When the car passed, she peeked at it. The green Porsche! For a moment she felt her heart pounding and again her throat ached. So Matt did care enough about her to check on her safety.

Care! Matt didn't know the meaning of the word. He was probably furious at her for leaving him so unceremoniously. Matt was not the type of man women walked out on. Right this minute he was probably on his way to see Jass. Or maybe he thought a trip into Houston might smooth over the fiasco with Lana.

Cara watched red taillights until she saw the Porsche turn onto the access road to the causeway, then she slipped back into the phone booth. No need for secrecy or hiding now. She closed the door and called a taxi.

The night sounds of the island seemed magnified as Cara waited for her ride to arrive. Tree frogs croaked. Somewhere a radio blared a disco tune. And always the sea slapped against the shore.

In a way I'm lucky, Cara said to herself. *I found out about Gwen in time to keep from making a complete fool of myself. It all adds up. The bill for a diamond solitaire from Neiman Marcus, the redecorating of Oleander House, Gwen. Of course Matt would put the beach house up for sale if his wife preferred living in a Victorian mansion. That's why*

*he was so angry when I mentioned that the stairway at
Oleander House reminded me of a wedding. I was
coming too close to his secret. Gwen's the girl who
will walk down that stairway in white satin—walk
down it to meet her bridegroom, Mathewson Daniels.*

"Taxi, lady? You call a taxi?"

Cara jumped. "Yes. Yes, I called you."

The driver got out and opened the rear door for
her. He was a plump, spare-tire-around-the middle
type who hardly gave her a second glance.

"Thank you," Cara murmured. "I appreciate your
promptness. Oleander House on Sealy Street,
please."

Cara sat well back in the corner of the back seat
wishing she could hide forever, ride away from all
her problems. But no. That was her dad's style, not
hers. She would face whatever was to come. She
breathed shallowly, trying to ignore the mingled
odors of fish and cigarette smoke and perfume that
clung to the upholstery in the cab.

When they reached Oleander House, Cara paid
the cabbie, adding a generous tip, then she hurried
through the wrought iron gate and up the steps to
the veranda. She paused in front of the door and
began pulling items from her purse one at a time,
groping for her key. Billfold. Calendar. Tissues. She
gave the purse a shake and heard the keys jingling
deep inside.

"May I be of help?" Matt stepped from the
shadows of the bougainvillaea vine that climbed on
the porch trellis.

Cara tried to hide her sudden fear behind the
anger that flooded through her.

"What are you doing here, Matt? Why are you

skulking about on my porch at this hour of the night?"

"*Your* porch?"

Cara felt her anger rise. The porch of Oleander House would never be her porch. Never. But Matt certainly didn't need to point out that fact to her. He didn't need to rub it in.

"My porch, using the term loosely, of course. My porch as long as my office is inside. I do hope I'm not disturbing you."

"Oh, come off it, Cara. What are you trying to prove?" Matt stepped forward, fitted his own key into the lock, and opened the door. "When I take a lady out for the evening, I always make it a point of honor to see her safely home. I'm glad you haven't completely denied me that privilege. Come, I'll see you upstairs to your quarters."

"That won't be necessary, Mr. Daniels."

"Whenever you call me, Mr. Daniels, I feel as if I've been sent back to square one."

"Perhaps you have." Cara kept her voice cool and even. "I believe that a more formal relationship will help facilitate the work we have to do on Oleander House."

"My, but aren't we businesslike!"

"I try to be." Cara started to step across the threshold, but before she could move, Matt picked her up bodily and carried her inside. She felt the warmth of his arms across her back and under her knees.

"Put me down! Put me down this minute, Matt!"

"What happened to Mr. Daniels?" Matt laughed, holding her tighter. "I'm sure Mr. Daniels was here just a second ago."

Cara kicked and pounded Matt's chest with her fists, but he paid no attention. He began climbing the stairs. She could feel his heart thudding against her cheek.

"Put me down before you have an attack," Cara demanded.

"Unlikely, though you could stand to lose a few pounds."

Cara started flailing with her fists again, but by this time they had reached her office door. Matt enclosed one hand around both her wrists, set her feet on the floor, then tilted her chin with his other hand and kissed her with the same gentleness he had displayed on their first meeting in the garden.

Caught totally off guard, Cara responded, enjoying the chills that feathered up and down her arms and legs. Matt released her wrists, but before she could decide what to do with her hands, he pinned her arms to her sides in an all-encircling embrace. Now his kiss grew demanding and Cara responded with a passion of her own that left her vulnerable and shaking when he released her. She wanted to stay in his arms, to be a part of him.

"Cara." Matt's soft voice was like another caress. "You love me. Why did you run away from me tonight?"

If she hadn't been shaking so badly, if she hadn't been so breathless, Cara would have admitted the truth. She would have blurted out to Matt that she loved him. She would have told him that she was insanely jealous of Jass and Lana and that she was sick at heart over the Gwen who in a few short months would be mistress of Oleander House. But her breathlessness locked the words inside her just long enough for her to notice that Matt was neither breathless nor trembling. If their kiss had done anything to throw him off-balance, he was hiding it.

"Cara, answer me. Why did you run off? I was frantic."

By repeating his question Matt had given her enough time to regain her composure. And her self-respect. What did he want? Did he expect to marry Gwen and still have fun and games with her?

"I left because I realized that you were playing on my emotions. I suppose you'll laugh at that since it took me so long to catch on."

"I think you're lying. You're making up a phony reason out of thin air and hot breath to put me on the defensive."

Cara began to shake again, angry because Matt could see through her so easily. But she held onto the few shreds of dignity left of her. She forced herself to remain silent, knowing that few people could stand silence.

"Why are you lying to me, Cara? What would you say if I told you I loved you?"

Cara felt her heart thump as if it might break her ribs. She couldn't control that inner reaction, but she could control her words. How like Matt to try to trick her! He hadn't said he loved her. Not at all. He had said—*what if*. She was glad she had caught the special wording. There was a lot of difference between a *what if* and a straight *I love you*.

"You're trying to use me, Matt." Cara repeated herself. "When you saw Jass at Sutton Place tonight you knew she would die of curiosity if we left so soon, didn't you? And that's exactly what you wanted. You wanted to arouse her curiosity. You enjoy keeping your women wondering and speculating about your actions."

"And you enjoy being theatrical and over-dramatic, hiding half-dressed behind potted palms, inviting party guests who are bound to cause double trouble, running off into the night without the slightest provocation. Perhaps you inherit your strong sense of theater from your father."

Cara closed her eyes to count to ten as she felt her fury mounting, but before she opened them, Matt was kissing her again—this time tenderly, gently. And this time Cara didn't respond. Except for the pounding of her heart she kept her cool until Matt released her.

"I hope you enjoyed that kiss, Matt. Because it was your very last one—from me. In the future our Oleander House discussions will be held during daytime business hours."

Matt stared at her for a long moment, then withdrew. "As you wish, Cara, good night."

Cara watched Matt walk slowly down the stairs before opening her door and closing it firmly behind her. She sensed that something between them had ended and she wasn't sure if she were glad or sorry.

Cara spent the next few days trying to keep too busy to think about Matt. She spent hours studying fabric swatches, carpet samples and wallpaper designs. She kept a notebook in which she drew up three tentative decorating schemes for each second-floor suite. The children's suite was the hardest and she saved it for the last.

"I'm not ready to look at your plans just yet," Matt said curtly when Cara called him at The Strand.

"All right, Matt. The six-month time limit on this project was your idea. You pick any time to go over the tentative plans that best suits your schedule. But I can do no more work until I have your decision regarding the bedroom suites."

"I don't want to see the plans until they're complete," Matt said.

Cara could sense Jass listening in on the third-floor extension and she flattened the impatience from her tone. "But the plans are complete. I have given you a multiple choice selection to consider for each suite."

"But we haven't visited Ashton Villa yet. Once you see it I know you'll want to make some changes and additions."

"When do you wish to tour the villa?"

"They will give us a special showing this afternoon at 4:30."

Cara bristled, but outwardly remained calm. "My business day ends at five, Matt."

"Then you'll just have to work overtime this once, I'm afraid. I'll call for you promptly at 4:15. Please be ready."

A click told Cara that their connection had been broken, but it was just as well. She was spluttering with indignation at Matt's high-handed manner and she would have hated him to know he had ruffled her composure.

That afternoon Cara was still angry. If Matt thought his late afternoon-into-evening date was going to lead to dinner afterward he was mistaken. She had no intention of letting him put her in a vulnerable position again. It was hard to look severely businesslike in pink, but when she dressed for her appointment with Matt she chose the most

tailored of her outfits from Mr. Gino, a suit with a
pencil-slim skirt. Although the day was warm, she
wore the jacket buttoned to the chin.

Matt called for her promptly at 4:15, but when
Cara reached the car she was surprised to find Jass in
the passenger seat. Jass had made every concession
to the weather. A scant knit top buttoned in a low V
in front left little to the imagination, and her slim
skirt fitted so snugly over her hips that only the bias
cut of the fabric kept the seams from giving.

"I've asked Jass to come along to take notes,"
Matt said as Cara settled herself on the back seat.
"That way you'll be completely free to concentrate
on the decor of the villa."

"How thoughtful of you, Matt." With great effort
Cara kept from grinding her teeth. She was furious
at Matt for choosing this pointed way of letting her
know that this was a nothing-but-business meeting.
How could she bear to have Jass chaperoning them!
Matt used people. It didn't matter who they were. If
they suited his purpose, he used them. And Jass
didn't even suspect a thing. Cara knew from the
gloating smile on Jass's face that Jass thought she
had made an important conquest.

When they reached Ashton Villa, Jass led the way
to the door. With each step Jass took the slit in her
slim skirt opened to reveal much knee and tanned
thigh. Cara tried not to mind that Matt had noticed
and was smiling.

"I want you to pay special attention to fireplaces
today, Cara. Oleander House has three fireplaces on
the second floor. I need your suggestions on refacing
them."

"Of course." Inside the villa Cara was dismayed to
note that the air conditioning wasn't working. She

walked beside Matt who was following Jass. She saw
the fireplaces without really seeing them at all. As
they toured the house she would leave a room and be
unable to remember what she had seen. But she
remembered well enough when Jass fanned herself
with her notepad and unbuttoned another button on
her knit top.

"I think buff brick complements an oak mantel,"
Matt said. "And I like either Norman or Roman
brick with polished walnut."

"I agree completely," Cara said. "You can't go
wrong with red brick and walnut."

The tour was endless. The warmer it got, the more
Jass seemed like the day's prime exhibit. Cara had to
restrain herself from giving an audible sigh of relief
when Matt suggested leaving.

"Jass, could you please type up your notes and
have them on Cara's desk first thing in the morning?"

"Of course, Matt."

Matt drove them back to Oleander House and Jass
left the car along with Cara. Cara went to her suite
thinking Matt would drive on, but he didn't. Obviously he was waiting for Jass to return. She adjusted
the louvers on her blinds to admit more breeze and
looked down into the garden. Matt was pacing off
distances between the old-fashioned wishing well
and the oleander bushes. He was so absorbed in his
counting that he was unaware of Jass approaching
directly behind him.

Jass must have spoken to Matt because Cara saw
him start before turning to face Jass. Cara could not
see Matt's expression in the shadowed twilight. She
watched Jass link her arm through Matt's and lead
him toward the wishing well. They stood for a

moment looking into the watery depths, then Jass hoisted herself to the stone rim of the well and leaned to one side in a way that brushed her breast against Matt's arm.

"Do you think it's a real wishing well, Matt?" Jass's throaty voice carried through the evening.

"I suppose any well is a wishing well if one has a wish."

"In that case I wish . . ." Jass's voice died away as she leaned again to look into the well. "Oh, Matt! I'm falling."

Cara watched Jass clutch wildly for support, one breast slipping from its mooring and the slit skirt revealing a knee to hip expanse of flesh. In a split second Jass's arms were around Matt, pulling his body to hers. Cara saw his muscled shoulders bulge under the thin fabric of his shirt as he lifted Jass safely to the ground, then her lips were on his.

Turning from the window Cara felt a mixture of emotions churning inside her. She felt disgust at Jass's cheap tactics. She was angry because she wasn't the one sharing Matt's kisses. But above all, she felt superior because she knew about Gwen. Jass could throw herself at Matt all she wanted, it was Gwen whom he loved. It was Gwen he would marry in January.

Chapter Ten

The next morning Cara was up early, determined to be prepared for Jass when she came in with her notes on Ashton Villa. She dressed carefully in a Mr. Gino pink skirt and sleeveless shell with a fragile gold chain at her neck. She worked at her desk for two hours with no interruptions before the telephone rang.

"Cara Logan. House of LaDeaux. Good morning."

"My, but don't we sound chipper today."

"Estelle! How are you? I was going to check on you a bit later in the morning."

"I'm fine, but I didn't call to discuss my health. I called to tell you I spent an interesting evening last night. Matt took me to a movie."

Cara was so stunned all she could say was "oh?" she had been so sure Jass had spent the evening with Matt that she could barely adjust her thinking.

"We saw a thriller based on a gothic romance and I want you to see it at your first opportunity. Are you free tonight?"

"I really don't care for movies, Estelle."

"Just go and note the interior settings. They're all turn-of-the-century and there are some classic examples of Victorian decor. Matt said he would love to take you but you insist on keeping eight to five office hours."

"Matt is right. I do. But if you think I'll benefit from seeing this movie, I'll attend it on my own time. Alone. Tonight."

"Fine, Cara. Call me tomorrow morning and let me know what you think of the ballroom decor in the last scene. I'll hold my opinion until I hear yours."

"Fair enough. And in the meantime you take care, Estelle." Cara was still staring at the telephone when Jass entered her office looking a bit hollow-eyed and pale.

"Good morning, Jass. You've brought the Ashton Villa material?"

"Yes. It's here." Jass laid the papers on Cara's desk, but she lingered. Had she expected Matt to be here?

"I really expected you earlier, Jass."

"Matt said I could take my time getting in this morning since last night . . ." Jass let her voice trail off suggestively.

"Last night was a late one?" Cara wondered what Jass was leading up to.

Jass yawned. "Matt and I had a wonderful time last night."

Cara pretended to read through the notes Jass had given her before looking up to smile reprovingly.

"You really shouldn't tell such lies, Jass. *You* may have had a wonderful time. And *Matt* may have had a wonderful time. But you certainly didn't have your wonderful times *together*. At least not last night."

"How do you know? You were home all evening."

Cara decided not to answer. It was all too absurd. If she had been friends with Jass she could have told her about Gwen so that she could at least save face by not continuing to throw herself at Matt. But she and Jass were not friends so Cara merely thanked Jass again for the Ashton Villa notes in a tone of dismissal.

Cara spent the rest of the day incorporating the ideas from Ashton Villa into her thinking, blending them with her own ideas, putting them through a subjective and creative mental process that even she couldn't analyze. All she understood of the process was the end result—ideas that were pleasingly fresh yet still Victorian in essence, ideas that were in no way a copy of what someone else had done.

When the phone rang, Cara was ready to quit work and go to the movie Estelle had asked her to view.

"Cara, I need a favor." Estelle's voice exuded enthusiasm as it flowed over the line.

"Of course, Estelle. What can I do for you?"

"I want you to go birding with me tomorrow. I'm going to try to take some pictures for the Pinkertons' second-floor bathroom. I have a wonderful idea for a mural, a seascape with herons in the foreground."

Cara squelched a groan. "Estelle really. I'm not into birds."

"I need your help, Cara. This is House of La-Deaux business. I have a new camera. A new tripod.

And frankly I need help in carrying all my equipment."

"All right, Estelle, I'll help. But has your doctor okayed these early-morning outings? They sound too strenuous to me."

"He said eight hours sleep and a nap. I'll retire early. Can you be ready by five?"

"Yes, of course. I'll be ready." Cara sighed as she replaced the receiver.

Cara attended the early evening movie, jotted a few notes, then retired, sleeping until her alarm rang in the dark predawn. Once she shut off the alarm she sensed an oppressive silence, but it wasn't until she stepped onto the veranda that she noticed the fog that cushioned the island like cotton batting.

When the car stopped, Cara hurried to it before she noticed it was Matt instead of Estelle.

"Get in," Matt said. "I don't like this any better than you do. But Estelle's not feeling well and she says she has to have those pictures. I promised to help her out."

"Then you don't need my help." Cara turned to leave.

"Get in," Matt ordered. "I can't manage the boat and all of Estelle's gear too."

Angrily Cara slipped onto the passenger seat and peered through the windshield. The fog was a gray monster swallowing the headlight beams.

"You'll never be able to see a bird in this fog, Matt."

Matt stepped on the gas, heading for Tiki Island.

"Estelle wants some closeup shots of the great blue herons, Cara. She has a new telephoto lens and a new tripod. And her camera has a built-in light meter. I think I can get the shots."

Matt drove slowly and by the time they reached Tiki Island Cara could make out the beach houses sitting like giant gray waterbugs on gray stilt legs. Gray. Gray. The whole world was like a globe of gray velvet. After parking in Matt's driveway he loaded Cara down with camera and beach bag before he grabbed binoculars, some flash attachments and the tripod and led the way toward the boatslip.

"The sun will soon burn off the excess fog," he said. He took his time motoring to the bird island, but even when they could make out the distinct outline of the sanctuary, fog still shrouded the whole area, giving palms and scrub pine a ghost-like appearance.

"I hear birds," Cara said. "They sound angry. Listen to that cluck-clacking. They probably hate this weather just as much as humans do."

"Who said anything about hating the weather?" Matt asked. "I like it. Let's see what the weatherman says." He snapped on the radio.

"Small craft warnings are in effect for the Port Arthur area. Rain is expected to continue. Small craft should stay in port. Winds are blowing at twenty to twenty-five miles per hour with gusts up to thirty-five miles per hour."

"I don't think we should stay out, Matt."

"Come on. We'll be back in less than an hour and we'll be within spitting distance from shore all the time. Those pictures are important to Estelle."

Cara agreed to this reluctantly, noting that although the regular tide was going out, a counter tide was coming in. White caps foamed on the water and the wind whooshed around their ears, blowing

Cara's hair back from her face and raising gooseflesh on her arms. The sun glowed dimly behind the cloud cover.

Matt maneuvered the boat in close to the bird sanctuary. "There's no point in trying to use the tripod in this chop, Cara. Just steady the camera the best you can. Hold your breath to eliminate body jiggle, then choose the quietest moment you can to snap the shutter."

"Great instructions, Matt. Now all we have to do is to find some herons." Cara tried to sight through the finder just for practice. "I can't see a thing."

"Let me take a look." Matt cut the motor, cast an anchor and eased forward, standing behind the seat where Cara sat. He adjusted a lens, then returned the camera to her. "Now try it." Matt sat down beside her as a few raindrops began pelting against the deck. Cara inched away from him, although her inclination was to ease closer to the protection his body offered.

"Matt, I'm frightened. Let's go in."

The boat rocked as a wave hit it broadside and for a moment Matt leaned toward Cara. He reached to steady her, then changed his mind and held to the gunwale instead. He started the motor and they sped back toward Tiki.

Now the rain was sheeting in torrents, and by the time Matt eased the boat into the slip and lashed it to the pilings Cara was soaked and shivering.

"Come on," Matt shouted. "Run for it!" He grabbed Cara's wrist, urging her along, but her ankle turned and she sprawled into sandy mud. She felt the grit scrape her elbows and her knees. She tasted it on her tongue and lips.

Cara had barely managed to pull herself to her feet when Matt swooped her into his arms. She tensed from anger and fright, then she realized she was safe in Matt's arms. She forgot her anger and her pride and basked in the warmth and strength he offered.

Pillowing her head against his chest she closed her eyes and counted the steps as he climbed to the house. Twenty-three. Twenty-four. Twenty-five. Now Matt stood on the deck. She could feel his strong heart pounding even through his heavy rain jacket. All her defenses dissolved in the lashing rain. She closed her eyes, half expecting Matt to kiss her, more than half wanting him to. But instead, Matt carried her inside and set her on her feet. When Cara opened her eyes, she was standing alone in the shower.

Angry that she again had been attracted by Matt's animal magnetism, Cara peeled off her soggy clothes. She shoved them into the far corner of the shower stall before she adjusted the flow of water to a pleasantly warm temperature. For several moments she just stood there enjoying the sensuous feeling of the spray massaging her chilled body.

"I hope you're saving some hot water for me," Matt called from somewhere in the hallway.

"I supposed you were the macho cold-shower type," Cara shouted back. She lathered her body and her hair with thick suds before she turned the water on again for a rinse.

Peeking from the shower stall to make sure the bathroom door was closed, Cara stepped onto a velvet-cut bath mat and grabbed a matching bath sheet from a rack. She toweled her body until she felt it glow, then she paused. She had nothing dry to slip into. She wrapped the bath sheet around herself and stepped into her bedroom. She was surprised to find no one there. She felt heat rise to her neck and face. What had she expected? Had she thought Matt would pounce on her the moment she emerged from the shower? And was she disappointed that he hadn't?

"There's a robe on the bed," Matt called. "Not exactly the kind you're used to, but try to make do."

Cara picked up the white terry cloth robe allowing her towel to slide to the floor. The robe was far too big, but she rolled the sleeves up, wrapped it around herself, and cinched it in at the waist with the wide sash. When she stepped into the hallway, Matt met her.

He had already showered and changed into brown slacks and an open-throated white shirt that contrasted with his golden tan. His thick mane of wavy hair was still damp and clung to his head in crisp waves. One unruly lock fell across his forehead, giving him a deceptively childish look. For a moment Cara was almost taken in by his look of innocence. But then common sense returned. He had probably practiced this scene many times and had learned that it got good reviews. Undoubtedly he had stood in front of a mirror carefully combing that lock of hair across his forehead.

"Not bad." Matt's eyes roved over Cara's figure, missing no detail. "But jersey is more your fabric. The terry cloth doesn't bring out the true you."

Cara ignored his remark. "I don't know how we're going to get home, Matt," she said looking through a picture window at the ever-worsening storm. Visibility was near zero and the outer world seemed to have been sprayed with wet pewter.

"You'll just have to stay here until Tropical Disturbance Dora lets up. I'll admit she came in faster than the weather forecasters predicted. And she'll probably hang around for a while. Tomorrow. The next day. The day after that."

"But I can't stay here that long—not for days. I have work to do, appointments to keep. And what will people think?"

"Then feel free to leave at any time. If my car wasn't up to its hubcaps in water, I'd be glad to drive you home."

Cara bristled at Matt's supercilious tone. How she wished she could splash off into the storm and leave him staring after her!

"Make yourself at home, Cara." His voice was mocking.

"Thank you. I will." Cara retreated into a bedroom, closing the door behind her. Now what? She couldn't stay holed up in here for the duration of a storm that could last for several days. She stretched out across the bed, staring at the ceiling and listening to the rain pounding against the roof.

Suddenly she was aware of the stealthy opening of the bedroom door. She jerked to a sitting position, clutching the bulky robe at the neckline where it tended to gape open. How dare Matt . . .

"Relax, Cara, relax. No need to defend your honor. I've merely come to collect your wet clothing for the laundry. You're wearing my favorite robe and I know you don't want to deprive me of its use any longer than necessary."

She watched as he picked up her sodden clothes,

examining her shirt and slacks, bra and panties. "Guess there's nothing here that can't stand a wash and a tumble dry, is there, Cara? And it is okay if I toss a few of my things in with yours, isn't it?"

Matt left with his soggy bundle, and Cara walked to the kitchen.

"The phone's out," Cara said when Matt returned. "I just tried to call out."

"You're stuck here, for the time being at least, unless you want to swim to Galveston. How about some breakfast?"

"I'll help you, Matt."

"Good. I thought perhaps the mystique of your career crusade precluded any such menial work."

The mystique of her career crusade indeed! Cara fumed. It was hard to show indignation while wearing a robe five sizes too large. She fried bacon and eggs while Matt mixed frozen juice in the blender and made buttered toast. They ate companionably at the breakfast bar, for a few moments forgetting the storm. As Matt cleared away their dishes they heard a strange squawking.

"What's that?" Cara turned to peer from the window. "Oh, Matt!" She pointed. "If we only had the camera ready now! It's a heron!"

They watched as the heron tried to fly into the wind. His huge wings were beating steadily, but an updraft caught him, carrying him straight up and then backward. The squawks continued until the wind slackened a bit and he was able to fly forward.

"First time I ever saw a bird fly backward." Matt peered at the heron until it disappeared into the gloom. "Hope he makes it home okay. Poor old fellow."

"Better save some sympathy for us. What about the hurricane shutters? Shouldn't you get them ready?"

Matt shook his head and continued gathering up coffee cups. "Winds are gusting to fifty miles per hour. That's far from hurricane force. I'll be able to lower the shutters quickly if the weather worsens, but I like to be able to watch a storm."

They watched the storm for most of the day. Cara tried to read. Matt paced, listening to the weatherband radio, then paced more.

Once he turned on some music and suggested dancing, but Cara vetoed that idea. She knew if their bodies touched again hers would melt. There was no one here to save her from herself. If it hadn't been for Gwen, she might have given in to the desire that made her blood run so hot.

Cara read. And when she looked up from her magazine, she saw Matt outside in swim trunks, leaning into the wind and walking toward the boatslip. The proverbial cold shower? Cara scowled. She flattered herself. His walk was unhurried and she could tell by the way he faced into the gale, that he was enjoying the storm. His tan swim trunks matched his skin so that from a distance he looked nude.

Cara suddenly wondered if Matt's body were tanned all over. There certainly were no telltale white lines at the waist and leg openings of his trunks. She flushed as she imagined him lying nude in the blazing sun. On the beach? On his boat? For the first time she wondered where Gwen lived. Surely not close by or Cara would have seen them together.

Matt checked the lines mooring the boat in the slip, and Cara watched the way his thigh muscles flexed. His arm and shoulder muscles worked in smooth coordination. Then he turned and waved at her, grinning like a schoolboy splashing in a forbidden puddle. How had he known she was watching?

Chapter Eleven

At lunchtime Cara made sandwiches. At dinner time Matt made a shrimp and spinach omelet. As Cara returned to the kitchen with their dishes the lights flickered and went out. Cara gasped and a spoon clattered to the floor.

"Don't panic," Matt said. "I have a supply of candles for just such emergencies." He lighted a bay-scented candle in a hurricane globe. A soft glow filled the room. "Very romantic, don't you agree?"

Matt was the only person Cara had ever known who showed style lighting a candle. It was something about the way he struck the match then flung it aside afterward. The thought occurred to her that Matt used women the same way he used matches, absorbing their brightness then casting them aside. Then suddenly Cara felt all her reserve melting away. "It is romantic, Matt. The storm really is beautiful when one gives in to it, relaxes and decides to enjoy it. It's almost as if its relentlessness pounds away frustrations and resentments."

All the arrogance left Matt's face. He studied Cara warily. She ate her omelet in silence, watching the way the candle glow highlighted Matt's hair and the cleft in his chin. She wished she were an artist so she could sketch him, catching the highlights of his prominent cheekbones and the rock-like jut of his jaw. How grand he would look sketched in charcoal on a porous white paper!

Why not enjoy Matt while she could? Clearly, he was no threat to her career now. Gwen had him wrapped up and packed in a box. Cara smiled to herself as she thought of other women who would like to be stranded in a storm with Matt Daniels.

After they had finished eating she cleared away their dinner things, helped Matt with the dishes, then sat down on the rattan couch and looked out across the bay. But there was nothing to see. Tiki Island lay in pitch blackness and only a few lights twinkled in the distance. To their left, Cara saw flames from the gas flares at refineries casting their red-orange glow against the clouds.

She could sense a watchful wariness in Matt. It was almost as if he were afraid of her. He didn't join her on the couch as she had hoped he would. He paced. He listened to the weatherband radio. He fixed them crème de menthe on the rocks. When he sat down, it was in his easy chair opposite the couch.

"If you don't mind, I thought we might discuss the decoration of the second floor at Oleander House. You did promise to have some fresh ideas ready for me today, didn't you? What have you decided to do about the children's suite?"

"Of course I have some fresh ideas, but I don't have my notes with me at the moment." There were six bedroom suites. Why had Matt elected to discuss the children's suite? Was he purposely reminding her that someone else would be the mother of his children? Gwen. Now Cara imagined Gwen in a new light. She couldn't picture Jass or Lana in a maternal role, but in her mind's eye Gwen began to materialize as a Botticelli-angel type, all dimples and soft sweetness.

"And are your ideas a secret?" Leaning forward Matt spoke in a tone which warned Cara that she had daydreamed through some other questions Matt considered important.

"Of course my ideas are not secret. In thinking of the children's quarters I'd like to point out that many bedroom suites depend on a mahogany or brass four-poster bed as the focal point of interest."

"A bit heavy for kids, don't you think?"

"Right. But I had in mind a practical variation on the four-poster theme. I'd like to see a frame the same size as the bed mattress, or perhaps just a bit larger, attached to the ceiling above a Hollywood style bed. The frame would be fitted with drapery pulleys and slides, and it would support a pleated draping of flowered sheets. These sheet-draperies could hang bunched at the four mattress corners in four-poster fashion. Or, they could be pulled to enclose the entire bed, turning it into a cozy private room within the larger room."

"That sounds as if it might delight the younger set." Matt smiled, and Cara wondered if he were imagining his own children.

"Go on," Matt said. "I like the pseudo four-poster idea. What have you planned to go with it?"

"The bedspread, which could be made of quilted sheets, and the hanging four-poster sheets would complement each other in design and color. One of the patterns would also be used as a wall covering."

"Sheets on the wall? Is that practical?"

"I think it is. Today's decorator sheets come in such wide widths that large expanses of wall can be covered with very little piecing or seaming."

"And just what holds the sheets to the wall?"

"Liquid starch. I've tried it. It works."

"It might work in Chicago, in a dry climate. But in Galveston with all its humidity, insects would be attracted to the starch. They'd literally dine on your wall covering for dessert."

"Not if salt is added to the starch. I've checked on that too. Sheet-covered walls are practical. If they get dirty, they can be taken down, laundered, and rehung. Or if one is tired of them, they can be put to their original use and something different can be used on the walls. Sheet fabric can also be used to cover toy shelves and closet accessories."

"Your plan sounds logical at that. Imaginative. The fabric design would have to be in keeping with the Victorian era."

"What colors do you have in mind, Matt? Pink? Blue?"

"How about a combination of the two?"

"Fine." Cara felt her throat grow tight. Did this man expect her to ask how large a family he was planning? She finished her drink and carried her glass to the kitchen.

"I believe I'll go to bed, Matt. Thank you for an excellent dinner."

"You're welcome. Let me know if you need

anything. And go ahead with your plans for the children's suite. Your ideas sound good."

Cara slept fitfully that night, getting up several times to get a drink or peer out the window. Was Matt sleeping soundly? Cara pictured him lying in bed, his lean body dark against pale sheets. Did he sleep on his back? His stomach? Or perhaps he slept as she did on one side. She imagined Matt in bed beside her, their bodies nestling together like silver spoons in a velvet case.

After a wakeful night, Cara overslept in the morning. When she came fully alert, she heard Matt moving about in the kitchen. She dressed quickly and joined him.

"Sorry I'm late," she murmured, stifling a yawn and watching the rain pour down.

"Yeah, it's too bad you overslept," Matt said. "You probably missed out on the first ten million raindrops of the day. Coffee?" Matt filled a mug and shoved it in front of Cara, then he slipped into a yellow slicker and rain hat, pausing to listen to the weather-band.

". . . decreasing winds. Rising flood waters are forcing people from their homes in some Galveston residential areas. All persons who own small boats are asked to join in the rescue operation to evacuate families and relocate them in approved shelters. I repeat—all persons with small boats are asked . . ."

Matt turned the volume down. "I'm going to help."

"Then how about taking me home?"

"No way."

"Why not, Matt? You could go near Oleander House. It's not in the flood area, but you could let me out close enough to walk home."

"I know that. But you are in no danger. You're safe. That gives you a non-emergency status. Be patient. You'll get back home soon enough." Matt stepped onto the storm-washed deck.

Cara could hardly contain her anger. Why did Matt want her here? He hadn't even come near her in the past twenty-four hours.

For a while Cara nursed another cup of coffee as she watched the storm. The rain had slacked off and the wind had died down, but the bay waters surged in a murky brown chop and the sun was nowhere in sight.

After a while she settled down with a book and became so engrossed in a chapter on hurricanes that she didn't hear Matt returning until his boat was right at the slip. She ran to the window. One look told her something was wrong. Two men were with Matt. They were helping him up to the house.

She dropped her book and ran to the door. The men helped Matt from the boat. One man eased his shoulder into Matt's right armpit to help him hobble to the steps while the other man followed carrying crutches and Matt's shoe. Matt heaved himself up the steps, using his helper as a human crutch and hopping on his left foot. When he reached the doorway, he turned to the men and Cara rushed out to take the crutches and Matt's right shoe.

"Okay, guys," Matt said. "I'll be fine. Use the boat as long as you need it." Matt watched until the men brought the boat about and pointed it back toward Galveston, then he turned toward the bedroom wing of the house. If Cara hadn't been there to offer support, he would have fallen. She had to brace herself on a chair to keep from going down under his weight.

"Matt! What happened? You need a doctor."

Matt threw his good arm around Cara's shoulder and she could hear him gritting his teeth. "Get me into my bed, please. I've already seen the doctor. Where do you think I got this sling and the crutches?"

Cara helped Matt to his bed and listened to his terse account of how he slipped while trying to rescue an elderly lady from her flooded living room, fell spraining his right ankle and dislocating his left shoulder.

"Doc says to stay in bed today and keep off the ankle for a week or so. Can't use but one crutch until the shoulder heals. Can you get me out of this slicker?"

Cara felt helpless as she looked at the pain in Matt's eyes.

"Can you ease forward?" She pulled the slicker from his left shoulder. "I'll grip the right sleeve and pull." Somehow they managed to get the slicker off, but Cara was dismayed to see that Matt's clothing was as soaked as the arm sling. Matt settled onto the bed and Cara propped pillows at his back. She pulled off his left shoe then lifted both his legs onto the bed.

"You should have been a nurse," Matt said. "Can you help me off with this wet shirt?"

Cara tried to work gently, but again she heard Matt grinding his teeth. At last the shirt came off and Matt lay bare from the waist up.

"Now the pants, please."

"Matt!"

"The pants, Cara. Now's no time for modesty. I can't lie here in these soggy khakis and I can't get them off by myself." Matt fumbled at his belt buckle, at the zipper, perspiration beading on his forehead.

"Let me do it, Matt. I'll look the other way."

"Do that. It's my prime concern."

Cara ignored his sarcasm as she peeled the soggy pants from Matt's waist and tugged them out from under his hips. Her fingers tingled when they accidentally brushed against his buttocks and thighs.

"Good work, Cara. Now grab the pant cuffs and pull—gently, please. Gently."

Cara eased extra pillows from a spare bed behind Matt's back, draped his terry cloth robe around his shoulders and helped him pull the sheet to his waist. When she left Matt's room, she was shaking. She knew then that she couldn't go on working for Matt Daniels. Her physical attraction to him was so strong it overpowered her reason. She had touched Matt in places she had touched no other man. She felt weak. She forgot his arrogance and egotism. She forgot everything but the strong feel of his arms about her, the warmth and passion of his kisses.

No she couldn't forget quite everything. She remembered Gwen. That was why she had to give up the Oleander House project. She couldn't bear working for a man she loved knowing he loved someone else.

Some time later Matt hobbled into the kitchen. He had managed to get into his robe. "Cara!" he exclaimed. "You're white as a tic bird. What's the matter?"

"I'm all right." Cara's throat could hardly force the words out. She needed to talk to Estelle. Would Estelle fire her? Or would she let her salvage some dignity by resigning? Cara knew she had to tell Estelle how she felt. And soon.

"Pour us some coffee," Matt said. "And relax. Sprained ankles and dislocated shoulders are painful, but they're seldom terminal. I'll be okay."

Cara gulped black coffee so hot it scalded her mouth. Almost immediately she broke out in a sweat. She stepped onto the deck to cool off. Now the sun was burning through the pewter-colored clouds, turning them to a creamy frog-belly white. The murky brown water was receding. It reached only midway on the cars' hubcaps. A helicopter circled overhead, looking like a giant mosquito as it surveyed the flood area. Cara returned inside.

"I want to go home, Matt."

"But that's impossible. Be reasonable. The phone's still out. Traffic won't be moving yet. And anyway, I'm going to need you here to help me. You can't just go off and leave me. I might starve."

He was playing on her emotions again. Darn the man! But she had to admit he had a point.

Somehow she got through the rest of the day. She cooked dinner, working from the store of food in Matt's small freezer. As soon as they finished eating she announced she had a headache and went to bed.

The heavy thumping of a crutch awakened her early the following morning but she didn't leap up to see if she could be of help. Let Matt fend for himself! But when she heard a dish break, she felt guilty. She dressed quickly. She mustn't let Matt overdo. As she walked across the deck she saw that wind and sun had dried the planked flooring. The sun glinted, a gold doubloon in a blaze of blue sky. Tiki Island smelled fresh and clean.

"Good morning, Cara," Matt called from the kitchen. "It's a beautiful day. I've been up since dawn and I got Estelle's heron picture right from the patio."

"Good," Cara said flatly. "Can I help with breakfast?"

"Won't be necessary," Matt said. "I'm up and about."

Cara steadied a stool at the breakfast bar as Matt heaved himself onto it, then she leaned his crutch against the counter where he could reach it easily. He was wearing the white terry robe. She tried not to look at the neckline where it gaped revealing an expanse of tanned skin and a covering of virile tawny hair.

The phone rang and Matt reached to scoop up the receiver. "Good. The phone's working again." Then he spoke into the receiver. "Matt Daniels speaking . . . Gwen! . . . What a surprise . . . Of course you're welcome. You know you're welcome anytime. When does your plane arrive? I can't meet you personally. We've had a storm here and there are still a few problems. But I'll send a car for you, okay? Take care yourself . . . Flight 901. Right? See you soon."

An inner glow lighted Matt's face as he replaced the receiver and looked at Cara. "Gwen's arriving at eleven on flight 901. Couldn't wait any longer to see Oleander House."

"I thought it was to be a surprise for her," Cara said.

"Afraid I leaked the surprise. I wanted her to have the fun of anticipating the finished product."

"But how are you going to meet her?" Cara asked, anger mounting as Matt now spoke of Gwen so openly.

"Half the freeway is open," Matt said. "Heard that on the news. I was hoping—I'll rent a car and—"

"You can't do that. The doctor said you were to take it easy. That drive in to Houston will be a mess. One-way traffic. Lots of truckers trying to make up for lost time. Maybe Jass could go." Cara squelched a sarcastic laugh.

"No. Jass has to keep on top of my warehouse affairs. This will be a full day for her." Now Matt looked at her pleadingly. "Cara, would you meet Gwen for me?"

She tried to think of a scathing refusal.

"You will go, won't you, Cara?" Matt asked again. "I know you're eager to finish the Oleander project on time, but I'll grant you a few days extension if necessary."

How did this man have the gall to ask her to meet his fiancée!

"Will you go, Cara?" Matt demanded. "You must!"

"In *these* clothes?" Cara looked down at the rumpled slacks and shirt she had been wearing for days. "And what would I use for transportation?"

"Gwen's not a fashion analyst," Matt said. "She'll understand about the clothes. And I'll rent a car. Will you go for me?"

Not for you, Cara thought. If I go it will be for Estelle and House of LaDeaux.

She held back her angry words. "Okay. I'll go."

Approximately half an hour later the driver from Rent-A-Car had arrived.

"You'll have to take the man back to his car lot, Cara." Matt hobbled to the deck door with her. "I really appreciate your doing this for me. Let me tell you what Gwen looks like so you'll recognize her."

Cara could no longer contain herself. She lashed out at Matt. At first her words came slowly, like catsup from a bottle, then more words followed in an angry torrent that she couldn't control.

"I'll meet Gwen at the airport, Matt. It's what any employee would do for her employer, isn't it? But you needn't describe Gwen for me. Spare me that, please. I'm fully aware of the type of woman you prefer. I'm sure your *fiancée* will dominate the entire Houston airport with her beauty and her charm."

"Cara!" Matt called to her, and for a moment she hesitated, but when she saw his mocking grin, she ran to the waiting rental car and slid onto the passenger seat without looking back.

Chapter Twelve

After the driver turned the car over to her at the Rent-A-Car lot, Cara drove to Oleander House and changed into a slim knit pantsuit and secured a matching hairband around her hair. She slipped into her sandals with the highest heels. So what if she was late meeting the plane! Let Gwen wait. She didn't intend to greet Matt's fiancée in an impromptu outfit that made her look like a frump. She checked her appearance in the mirror, pleased with the way the apricot hairband brought out a near blush color in her olive skin.

The drive to Houston took longer than she had expected. One half of the freeway was closed and she was unused to facing head-on traffic in the next lane. In some spots muddy water still lapped to the edges of the freeway. In adjacent pastures cattle stood knee deep in water or mud. Here and there tic birds perched on protruding knobs of dry land, animated blobs of whipped cream on a sea of chocolate pudding.

Traffic was heavy at the airport. The closest parking place was almost a block from the terminal. Cara's feet ached by the time she threaded her way through the crowd to the flight 901 baggage claim area. The luggage carrousel was turning, but no bags appeared on the conveyor belt yet. For several moments Cara stood back and studied the crowd, then she approached an elderly lady.

"Do you know if flight 901 has landed yet?"

"Yes, Miss. My grandson was aboard. That's him there in the green shirt and jeans." She smiled proudly at the boy's broad back.

Cara smiled and looked back at the crowd. Which of these women was Gwen? The flashy brunette in the see-through blouse? No. She was clinging to a man's arm. The blonde in the red suit? No. She had a toddler clutching her skirt. Cara gulped. Maybe Gwen was a divorcée. Maybe that child was the reason for the children's suite.

Now the baggage began to arrive and the crowd pushed closer to the carrousel. Cara stood waiting until the crowd thinned out. At last only three women remained, a healthy-apple type wearing a tailored dress and chunky gold jewelry, a tall willowy girl dressed in white and carrying a tennis racket and a petite, middle-aged lady with caramel-colored hair that matched her tailored suit.

Stepping to an information desk, Cara spoke to the girl in charge. "Could you page a passenger from flight 901 for me?"

"Yes. The passenger's name, please?"

"Gwen—" Cara hesitated, realizing she didn't even know Gwen's last name. "Just say Matt Daniels is paging Gwen."

The girl grinned at her, but she repeated the message into a loudspeaker. "Matt Daniels paging Gwen. Will Gwen please come to the information desk?"

Cara was amazed to see the middle-aged lady approach the desk.

"Gwen?" Cara asked tentatively. "Mrs. Daniels?"

The lady smiled up at Cara. "Yes. I'm Gwen Daniels. And you're—"

"Cara. Cara Logan." Cara felt herself shaking again, felt anger rising in a hot flood. "I work for House of LaDeaux and for Mr. Daniels."

"Why, of course. You must be the Cara Matt has mentioned so often in his calls and letters. I'm eager to hear about your latest plans for Oleander House." Gwen stopped speaking and frowned slightly. "Are you all right, dear? You seem quite flushed. Perhaps a cool drink before we start off . . ."

"I'm fine, Mrs. Daniels." Cara inhaled deeply, trying to calm down. "If you're ready, why don't we head back to Tiki? Matt's will be eager to see you." Cara carried one bag for Gwen, glad for an outlet for some energy that might work off part of her anger. Yet why was she angry? Matt had said he was preparing Oleander House for his mother. Estelle was the one who mentioned a fiancée. If only she had considered the possibility that Matt called his mother by her first name! Why *hadn't* she thought of that? She called her own dad Hank, didn't she?

Cara chewed on the inside of her cheek. There

was no way she could blame Matt for her angry outburst as she left Tiki that morning. How could she ever face him again!

Once they reached the car and settled down for the ride back to the bay area Gwen kept up a steady conversation.

"I've always loved the old Victorian mansions in Galveston," she said. "Matt has made my long-time dream come true by buying Oleander House for me."

"That's nice. I love decorating a house for someone who really appreciates the end results."

"Are the gardens still intact?"

"Oh, yes. It'll take a landscape person to bring them back to their original beauty, though. Landscaping is a bit out of my line." Cara wanted to question Gwen about the children's suite at Oleander House, but she couldn't bring herself to do so. She couldn't bear to hear Gwen speculating about future grand-children or about Matt and his girl friends.

Gwen chattered, listened, then chattered some more, and at last they reached Tiki Island and the beach house. Care helped Gwen gather her things, helped her by carrying one bag up the steps to the deck. Then before she had to face Matt, she retreated to the rental car and sped off toward Galveston.

Once home Cara flung herself across her bed. She vowed not to cry although hot tears stung her eyelids. No man was going to reduce her to tears! Yet it was really not Matt's fault, she realized miserably. Her own jump-to-conclusions foolishness had made her spout off to Matt.

There was nothing left for her to do but to resign, to leave Oleander House and Galveston as quickly as she could. Estelle could find a replacement for her. There were plenty of eager young decorators fresh out of school who would jump at the chance to work for House of LaDeaux.

When the telephone rang, Cara was tempted to ignore it or to lift the receiver off the hook and lay it aside indefinitely. But she couldn't do that. Estelle might need her.

"Cara Logan speaking."

"Cara!" Estelle said. "The phone rang for so long I was beginning to think you weren't there and—"

"Estelle, I want to apologize."

"But whatever for, Cara?"

"Please hear me out. I've made a fool of myself in front of Matt and I'm sorry. I've loved working on the Oleander House project, but under the circumstances I can't continue. I—"

"Cara, save whatever it is you're trying to tell me for another time, okay? Matt called me out to Tiki to meet Gwen. She wants a tour of Oleander House immediately. She's dying to see it from top to bottom. I'm sending her over to you in a taxi."

"Estelle, please listen to me. I simply can't go on working with Matt. There's absolutely no way. I'm packing to leave."

"Oh, Gwen's not afraid of a little mess, Cara. She just wants an overall view of the house. She's tired from her trip, but she's dying to see Oleander House today."

"Estelle! We must have a bad connection. I'm trying to tell you that I'm leaving. Resigning. I'm leaving within the hour." Cara heard her voice shrilling, her words tumbling over each other, but she could neither slow down nor speak more quietly. "Of course I'll leave the pink costumes here for your next girl. Maybe she'll be my size. I'll leave all my notes and the estimates. Everything is in good order. You'll be able to pick up where I've left off. You'll be able to find someone to finish up the project. And you can tell Matt Daniels I said it wouldn't hurt to allow your next girl an extra month."

"You will meet Gwen on the front veranda in about five minutes, won't you, Cara? She wants to see the garden first. I've been telling her about the wishing well and—"

"Estelle! No! Listen to me."

"Wonderful, Cara. I really appreciate this. I know you've had a hard few days and it's good of you to give this extra bit of yourself for your client. Gwen will be right there."

Cara stared at the receiver. How dare Estelle do this to her! Unfair! Cara jerked her suitcase from the closet, slammed it onto her bed, and flung it open. Then she paused. Guiltily she admitted to herself that she was the one being unfair. She was placing her reaction to her misplaced love for Matt ahead of her loyalty to Estelle. Oleander House wasn't merely her project. The project was one of many that concerned House of LaDeaux. Any employee owed her employer ample notice before quitting, no matter what the circumstances.

Reluctantly Cara replaced the suitcase in the closet, straightened her suite and walked very slowly down to the veranda. In moments Gwen arrived. When she heard Gwen ask her driver to wait, she relaxed a bit. Surely the tour would be short if the taxi meter was running.

"Cara, I know this is an imposition," Gwen called

out as she hurried toward the porch. "It's wonderful of you to be so willing to show me the house. Matt told me what a time the two of you have been having the past few days. If Matt weren't so crippled . . ."

Cara stepped forward, meeting Gwen before she reached the veranda steps. "I'm delighted to show you the place, Mrs. Daniels. Estelle said you wanted to start with the gardens. I'm afraid they'll be a disappointment to you, they're so overgrown."

"I have a keen imagination. I always try to see things as they could be."

See things as they could be! Had Gwen guessed that Cara loved Matt? Surely the truth wasn't etched on her forehead. But maybe Matt told her about the angry scene before Cara drove to the airport.

Cara led the way around the old mansion, shoving aside branches, pointing out the wishing well and the blooming oleanders. She took great pains to keep her manner very professional.

"I can hardly wait to get my pruning shears and my weed eater in here," Gwen said. "I'm really glad this outdoor area isn't your concern, Cara, because I'm going to make it mine. I want to put something of myself into this place, and even my enemies admit I have a green thumb."

"You plan to do all the landscaping yourself?"

"Oh, absolutely. But with Matt's help, of course. I'll need his strong muscles, but he won't mind. Matt loves to work with growing things."

They circled the grounds and when they came back to the well Cara urged Gwen toward the veranda. "Let's go inside, Mrs. Daniels. There's not much more to see out here."

Cara led the way into the house, reciting her plans for the first floor.

"I can see it all in my mind, Cara. The unifying claret color, the fabrics, the polished walnut. I find your ideas very impressive. I can hardly wait to see them carried out."

Gwen's enthusiasm was contagious, and Cara felt a sudden reluctance to leave the Oleander House project. She had a strong desire to finish what she had started. But impossible! Her feelings toward Matt made her staying on out of the question. Cara ushered Gwen to the second floor, pointing out her own suite, then the other suites.

"I love all the fireplaces," Gwen said. "I want each of them in proper working order."

"Of course," Cara said. "Matt mentioned that too. I'm in the process of getting estimates on their repair."

"Which of the suites will be decorated for the children?" Gwen asked.

Cara hid her hurt deep inside herself as she showed Gwen the children's suite and explained her decorating plan. When she finished, Gwen beamed at her.

"Perfect, Cara. I can see it in my mind right now. Josie and Marty will love the four-poster sheet effect."

"Josie and Marty?"

"My granddaughters—my daughter's girls in New York. The only way I could get them to let me return to Galveston was to promise them their own room and a long visit each summer."

Again Cara felt foolish. Why hadn't she thought of the possibility that Gwen already had grandchildren! But what did it matter now? She was leaving. She would like to finish the project, but she could not bear working with Matt even a day longer. She had made a fool of herself. She had fallen in love with an impossible man. Now it was time to leave.

Gwen took a quick look at the ballroom, spoke briefly to Jass, then thanked Cara for the tour. Cara walked with her to the taxi, then she returned to her suite and sat down to think.

Two weeks. She would have to give Estelle two weeks notice. That was only fair. She would force herself to be civil to Matt for those two weeks, then she would return to Chicago, find a department store job and forget about Galveston. And Matt.

Cara had just slipped into her robe and was running a tub when she heard a thumping in the outer hallway. Turning off the water she ran to her office and flung open the door.

"Matt! Are you trying to kill yourself?" She rushed down the stairs to help Matt.

"I can manage. Just give me room and keep out of my way."

Cara stood by helplessly while Matt made a painful ascent. As soon as he caught his breath he picked up the telephone and dialed. "Jass? Please report to the warehouse and close my office there for the day. Then you may go home. Take the rest of the afternoon off."

"Very generous of you, Matt." Cara glanced at her watch. "It's almost five o'clock."

Matt eased himself down on Cara's couch. "That's all right. I want to talk to you and I don't want any interruptions. What's all this Estelle's telling me about your resigning your position? You have a contract, you know. You have an obligation—"

"It's just as she's told you, Matt. I was a bit hasty when I broke the news to her. I'll give her ample notice of my leaving—two weeks. But I am going, contract or no contract."

"You're quitting? Walking out?" Matt balanced his crutch across his knees. "I thought you were built of sterner stuff."

"I realize I owe you an apology. And I do apologize. It was very unprofessional of me to throw such a tantrum over picking Gwen up. I'm sorry." For a moment Cara felt proud of herself for keeping just the right amount of aloofness in her voice.

"You're in love with me, Cara. Why don't you admit it? You're in love with me and you're afraid of your own emotions so you're running away. Admit it."

"I won't admit what isn't true. If I ever fall in love with any man, it certainly won't be with a conceited, arrogant—"

"Hold it. Hold it. Don't say things you'll regret." Matt grinned at her in a maddening way. "For a while you had me convinced that you hated me. When you didn't respond to that last kiss, when you kept insisting that we keep our meetings strictly business. I almost gave up on ever winning you over, Cara. But actions speak louder than words."

"What do you mean?" Cara pulled her robe more tightly around herself, trying to ignore Matt's appreciative gaze. How she wished she had never purchased the robe!

"I mean that you wouldn't have been so angry about my *fiancée*, Gwen, if you didn't care about me," he said smugly.

"You're wrong."

"I'm right. You're just mixed up, Cara. Think. I've told you I love you. You've shown me that you love me. Can't we—"

"You've never told me you love me, Matt. Never." Cara pressed her lips into a thin line to stop their trembling.

"But I did tell you I love you. I can recite the exact time and place."

"You said, *'What if* I told you I love you.' That 'what if' made all the difference in the world. I see through your tricks. You're trying to use me to get a good decorating job on Oleander House. You use everyone. You've used Jass to get top secretarial work. You've used Lana for business reasons."

Matt's smile turned into an infuriating chuckle. "Jass was an efficient secretary long before I began dating her, Cara. And my dates with Lana have only been business appointments. Even the party was business-oriented. I've dated a lot of girls in my life, Cara, but I've never told any of them I loved them. I've been saving those words for you. I've been waiting until I found the right girl."

Matt's words held a ring of truth, but Cara refused to admit it to herself. "Jass. Lana. All those women! And for whom did you buy that engagement ring?"

Now Matt sat straighter and leaned forward, a puzzled expression on his face. "What engagement ring, Cara?"

"Don't play innocent! I accidentally found a Neiman Marcus receipt for a diamond solitaire in a drawer at your penthouse."

Matt grinned broadly and held out his right hand. "The receipt was for the repair of this ring, Cara. It's a family heirloom, the only small memento I have to remember my father by. I've always loved it."

Cara flushed as she realized she had made another error. "No doubt wearing such a grand diamond makes you feel very important," she said coldly. "I can't stand your big ego, Matt. Anyone who can bask in the glitter of a diamond, anyone who can look at the sea and feel *important* . . ."

"You never did let me explain what I meant about the sea. I won't retract my words. The sea does make me feel important because it is so vast, because it's such a great part of a great universe. When I look at the sea, I feel important because I know that I'm a part of that universe too. I belong—I'm important because I'm a tiny part of all that greatness."

Cara looked at Matt in surprise as she considered the truth of what he had just said. Perhaps she was the one who was egotistical. The sea made her feel small because she was thinking only of herself and not of her relationship to the universe or to others in the universe. She was silent as she considered what Matt had said. At last she spoke.

"Matt, maybe I've been wrong. Maybe I've misjudged both of us."

"Making faulty judgments is an easy thing to do in these complicated times." Matt sighed. "We're all too easy on ourselves."

"What do you mean?" Now Cara sat down beside Matt ready to listen, ready to try to understand whatever it was he was about to say.

"I mean that we all tend to grasp at the few things in life that we can control. Usually material things. Our clothes. Our cars. Our homes. Then we're disappointed. Things that used to signify great success no longer do so. A private pool. Two cars in the garage. A well-equipped modern home. But the people who achieve them aren't satisfied. They feel cheated, unfulfilled. I know. I've been there."

"Life promised rib eye and delivered eggplant. Is that what you're saying?"

"In a way, but not entirely. We need to be hard on ourselves, Cara. We need to see beyond the pool and cars and clothes. We need to determine our basic values. We need to seek out the quiet things that are worth living for."

"Things like blue herons and oleanders and . . ."

"And love, Cara. I love you. I want to marry you. I want to see you walk down this staircase here wearing white satin and lace."

Matt held out his arms to Cara and she melted into them. "I love you, Matt. We'll be married the minute Oleander house is finished. I'll give up my career and—"

"Hold it. Who said anything about giving up your career?"

"But—but—I thought you wanted—"

Matt reached into his pocket and pulled out a business card and handed it to Cara. She read aloud.

"Daniels Building Supply—Decorating by House of LaDeaux."

"We'll be partners in more ways than one, Cara. Do you like the idea?"

"Matt, you are an arrogant, egotistical, conceited—"

"Love," Matt finished. He pulled Cara to him and this time she didn't resist. When she was in Matt's arms, it was like looking at the sea. She became a part of the greatness.

15-Day Free Trial Offer
6 Silhouette Romances

6 Silhouette Romances, free for 15 days! We'll send you 6 new Silhouette Romances to keep for 15 days, absolutely free! If you decide not to keep them, send them back to us. You pay nothing.

Free Home Delivery. But if you enjoy them as much as we think you will, keep them by paying the invoice enclosed with your free trial shipment. We'll pay all shipping and handling charges. You get the convenience of Home Delivery and we pay the postage and handling charge each month.

Don't miss a copy. The Silhouette Book Club is the way to make sure you'll be able to receive every new romance we publish before they're sold out. There is no minimum number of books to buy and you can cancel at any time.

This offer expires September 30, 1982

Silhouette Book Club, Dept. SBN 17B
120 Brighton Road, Clifton, NJ 07012

Please send me 6 Silhouette Romances to keep for 15 days, absolutely free. I understand I am not obligated to join the Silhouette Book Club unless I decide to keep them.

NAME_____

ADDRESS_____

CITY_____STATE_____ZIP_____

IT'S YOUR OWN SPECIAL TIME

Contemporary romances for today's women.
Each month, six very special love stories will be yours
from SILHOUETTE. Look for them wherever books are sold
or order now from the coupon below.

$1.50 each

Hampson	☐ 1 ☐ 4 ☐ 16 ☐ 27 ☐ 28 ☐ 40 ☐ 52 ☐ 64 ☐ 94	Browning	☐ 12 ☐ 38 ☐ 53 ☐ 73 ☐ 93
Stanford	☐ 6 ☐ 25 ☐ 35 ☐ 46 ☐ 58 ☐ 88	Michaels	☐ 15 ☐ 32 ☐ 61 ☐ 87
		John	☐ 17 ☐ 34 ☐ 57 ☐ 85
Hastings	☐ 13 ☐ 26 ☐ 44 ☐ 67	Beckman	☐ 8 ☐ 37 ☐ 54 ☐ 72 ☐ 96
Vitek	☐ 33 ☐ 47 ☐ 66 ☐ 84		

$1.50 each

☐ 5 Goforth	☐ 29 Wildman	☐ 56 Trent	☐ 79 Halldorson
☐ 7 Lewis	☐ 30 Dixon	☐ 59 Vernon	☐ 80 Stephens
☐ 9 Wilson	☐ 31 Halldorson	☐ 60 Hill	☐ 81 Roberts
☐ 10 Caine	☐ 36 McKay	☐ 62 Hallston	☐ 82 Dailey
☐ 11 Vernon	☐ 39 Sinclair	☐ 63 Brent	☐ 83 Hallston
☐ 14 Oliver	☐ 41 Owen	☐ 69 St. George	☐ 86 Adams
☐ 19 Thornton	☐ 42 Powers	☐ 70 Afton Bonds	☐ 89 James
☐ 20 Fulford	☐ 43 Robb	☐ 71 Ripy	☐ 90 Major
☐ 21 Richards	☐ 45 Carroll	☐ 74 Trent	☐ 92 McKay
☐ 22 Stephens	☐ 48 Wildman	☐ 75 Carroll	☐ 95 Wisdom
☐ 23 Edwards	☐ 49 Wisdom	☐ 76 Hardy	☐ 97 Clay
☐ 24 Healy	☐ 50 Scott	☐ 77 Cork	☐ 98 St. George
	☐ 55 Ladame	☐ 78 Oliver	☐ 99 Camp

$1.75 each

☐ 100 Stanford	☐ 105 Eden	☐ 110 Trent	☐ 115 John
☐ 101 Hardy	☐ 106 Dailey	☐ 111 South	☐ 116 Lindley
☐ 102 Hastings	☐ 107 Bright	☐ 112 Stanford	☐ 117 Scott
☐ 103 Cork	☐ 108 Hampson	☐ 113 Browning	☐ 118 Dailey
☐ 104 Vitek	☐ 109 Vernon	☐ 114 Michaels	☐ 119 Hampson

$1.75 each

6 brand new Silhouette Special Editions yours for 15 days—Free!

For the reader who wants more...more story...more detail and description...more realism...and more romance...in paperback originals, 1/3 longer than our regular Silhouette Romances. Love lingers longer in new Silhouette Special Editions. Love weaves an intricate, provocative path in a third more pages than you have just enjoyed. It is love as you have always wanted it to be—and more —intriguingly depicted by your favorite Silhouette authors in the inimitable Silhouette style.

15-Day Free Trial Offer

We will send you 6 new Silhouette Special Editions to keep for 15 days absolutely free! If you decide not to keep them, send them back to us, you pay nothing. But if you enjoy them as much as we think you will, keep them and pay the invoice enclosed with your trial shipment. You will then automatically become a member of the Special Edition Book Club and receive 6 more romances every month. There is no minimum number of books to buy and you can cancel at any time.

Silhouette Romance

Coming next month from
Silhouette Romances

Reluctant Deceiver by Dorothy Cork

When Merlyn flew to Hong Kong under false pretenses,
her plan backfired. Sullivan, the only man she would
ever love, refused to believe in her innocence.

The Kissing Time by Jean Saunders

When Julie is hired as Vince's research assistant, she
learns that when the gorse is in bloom on the Scottish
tundra, it is indeed, "the kissing time."

A Touch Of Fire by Ann Major

When Helen Freeman books a room in a Paris hotel she
finds that a handsome stranger has prior claim to it and
he intends to take full advantage of their
impromptu introduction.

A Kiss And A Promise by Anne Hampson

After Judith broke her engagement with Alexis she
thought their love had died. But when she went to live
in his house as a nanny to his young nephew, she
discovered that love can be rekindled.

Undercover Girl by Carole Halston

Reporter Kelly Lindsay was thrilled at the prospect of living
undercover in Palm Beach. But she had never imagined
that she would fall in love with the subject of her exposé!

Wildcatter's Woman by Janet Dailey

After years of divorce, Veronica realized that Race was the
same irresponsible wildcatter she'd walked out on—but
he also hadn't lost his heart-stoppingly powerful,
sensual magnetism.

**Look for *Daring Encounter* by Patti Beckman
Available in June.**

READERS' COMMENTS ON SILHOUETTE ROMANCES:

"I would like to congratulate you on the most wonderful books I've had the pleasure of reading. They are a tremendous joy to those of us who have yet to meet the man of our dreams. From reading your books I quite truly believe that he will someday appear before me like a prince!"

—L.L.*, Hollandale, MS

"Your books are great, wholesome fiction, always with an upbeat, happy ending. Thank you."

—M.D., Massena, NY

"My boyfriend always teases me about Silhouette Books. He asks me, how's my love life and naturally I say terrific, but I tell him that there is always room for a little more romance from Silhouette."

—F.N., Ontario, Canada

"I would like to sincerely express my gratitude to you and your staff for bringing the pleasure of your publications to my attention. Your books are well written, mature and very contemporary."

—D.D., Staten Island, NY

*names available on request